The Eye

of Set

By G.S. Christopher

A Sidewalk Labs Creation.
Palm Bay, FL, USA.

For information about this work and others contact:
publisher@sidewalklabs.net
or visit
www.sidewalklabs.net

First Edition v2. August 2016.

PART ONE

The Skeleton
& the Crown

It was the power of God.

It was a dissonance in his soul, to have no faith, but to encounter the omniscience, to know things, to change things. With the golden helmet on his head, these infinite eyes, eyes with vision as long as Time, history was painted on the magnificent canvas of his own experience. His blood pounded and boiled, adrenaline burned through his veins with an inhuman itch. He pressed his fingers lightly but surely to the cold lenses and walked through the veil. He stood between times. He lived outside the matrix of death; it could not follow him on this path. If there was fear, he didn't recognize it. If there was doubt, a call for hesitation, he did not succumb. With the helmet on his head, enlightenment was in his hands. It was his to ask and to receive.

Rick grinned the fierce and unapproachable grin of one who had escaped the Law.

He knew when he returned, when he removed the helmet from his head – chased away by the Shadow, or by his own human weakness – he would wonder at himself in the mirror, counting wrinkles, marveling, smiling at how few marred his face, after so much had been seen.

Later, as he drifted to sleep, he would feel the grin fade. He would sleep like we all do, with restless dreams that in time would force him into waking.

He shaved extravagantly; he put on his navy blue blazer and brushed it smooth down to the waist; he straightened his glasses carefully. Then, humming the strains of Vivaldi's "Spring," he left his flat and walked the short distance to the college campus. The lecture hall was on the other side of the grounds, but he gave himself plenty of time to spare. He took the path behind the tennis courts, a wooded area where students rarely ventured.

A swirl of breeze whistled through the leaves, and for a moment he felt a chill that caused him to stop in his tracks, shivering. It was an inexplicable cold, defying both the warm sun and the heavy blazer. It was the kind of chill that made one think of ghosts and graves, and he frowned as the mood suddenly changed, as worries made their presence felt but would not define themselves.

In that moment, as though called into existence by the anxious wind, a girl sitting on the bench by the tennis court came to his attention. He saw her before she noticed him. She was lost in a paperback, but when he started walking again she heard his footsteps on the path and looked up with a start, her wide innocent eyes like a frightened doe that heard the tread of the hunter. It made him feel guilty, out of place, that he had violated her pastoral peace. He stopped again, with a shyness far from his usual nature. They regarded each other, both wary but strangely unguarded, their faces sympathetic mirrors of antisocial introversion, eyes alert and lips pursed, each unable to hide their initial displeasure. But she made an effort to smile, and he stirred himself to return it as he continued walking toward her bench.

She did not go back to her book but instead watched as he approached. Though he wore nothing fancier than the blazer and tie, he felt over-dressed. It was only because she herself seemed so appropriate for the scene, he thought, her dress a pattern of earth tones that bled uninterrupted into the autumn foliage behind her.

He tried to think of a greeting with no success, and instead merely nodded an acknowledgment. She returned it with the slightest hint of amusement. He thought she must see his shyness plainly. He had at first thought her the same, but her quick, measuring look told him that while she was solitary, she was unafraid of the wildness of men.

It was because she was young, he told himself, where he had seen too much, lived too long to remain simple.

The path, and he on it, passed within feet of her. She looked back down at the book, as though to continue reading, but then her head came up again and she said, "You're Professor Mayliss, is that right?"

It did not come out so much as a question as a fact seeking confirmation. In the girl's tone was the same character he had seen in her eyes, a boldness, an assurance that invigorated her slight frame. He nodded, wondering if he should recognize her, if she was a student in one of his lecture classes. He could not place her. He said, "Yes, have we met?"

"No," she said. "I'm Rachel." Her grin widened as though that were cause for a laugh, but then her expression changed to one of concern when she

6

noticed his reaction. "Hey," she said, "are you all right?"

"It's nothing," Rick said, but that name – Rachel – would always be a punch to the gut. He composed himself quickly; he had no desire to go into long and painful explanations. He rushed into a question instead, to fill a silence that seemed longer than it was. "Are you a student?" But it was obvious she was, and as soon as he said it, he felt a fool.

"Grad student," she said, "second year." She closed her book and stood up, offering him a hand. There was something old-fashioned, even genteel in the gesture, and he took it gently, holding it delicately for a brief moment, not shaking it like he would a man's. "Your lecture is today?" she said. "I was considering attending."

"You study physics?" Rick said. She had struck him for some reason as an art student, or literature.

"Mathematics," she said matter-of-factly. "Numbers are my passion."

"An unusual passion," Rick remarked.

"I'm an unusual person," Rachel responded, in the same matter-of-fact tone. "Do you have a favorite?" She changed subjects abruptly. "Number, I mean."

"My favorite number?" he repeated.

She laughed. "Yes. Do you not have one?"

He said, "I've never really thought about it."

"Think about it."

He did, both of them standing next to the bench, and for a moment he no longer felt awkward, because she too was strange, and in their shared strangeness they had become comfortable. Finally, he said, "Phi," and shrugged. Take it or leave it.

"That's a good answer," she said, nodding slowly. "Golden ratio."

"Right."

"Pi would have been good," she said. "Phi is even better." He felt unaccountably pleased with himself, but then she said. "A little pretentious though, right?" He didn't have a response, and after a moment she clarified: "I mean, you picked it because of its artistic and philosophical implications, right? Trying to pick a number with *meaning*, isn't that what you were doing?"

He shrugged. "I don't know why I picked it." You made me, he thought but didn't say.

"It's not even really a number," she went on. "I mean, it shouldn't count." She thought back over what she had said and grinned when she realized she had made a pun. "It *can't* count, so it *shouldn't* count. Get it? It's irrational. That makes it a *function*, if you ask me. Kind of diminishes the whole idea to call it a number. Like it can be *counted*!" She laughed as if this was the greatest joke, and Rick grinned with her, thinking,

She's a nerd. She did not look it. Or maybe she was just showing off. Of course she had recognized him and knew who he was; he thought, she wants to seem intelligent.

"You're right," he said. "My new favorite: 26."

"26?" she repeated.

"My birthday," he explained. "February 26."

"You're a Pisces."

"Yes," he said after a moment, again feeling uncomfortable. She suddenly seemed very young to him, again, but not in a fresh, innocent way, more in the ignorant way of a child. He could not explain the change of mood. A moment from his youth came to mind, when he had bested a girl in a spelling bee. He could not have been more than ten years old. It had come down to just the two of them, and they had exchanged several words, and with each successive round he had seen how the girl had become more enamored of him. After losing, she had mystified him with a heartfelt smile of congratulations, as though she were as pleased by his victory as he was. It had soured the moment in a way he hadn't understood, with a taste of guilt he could not reconcile with the pride of winning. There was something wrong with the girl, he had decided – normal people did not like losing.

Rachel gave him an odd look, no doubt aware of his sudden inexplicable resentment. Her confusion made it worse. Did she need his approval? It reminded him she was merely a student, and he a professor. He looked at his watch dramatically, preparing to excuse himself, but she immediately said, "You need to get to your lecture? May I walk with you?" And he had no polite way of refusing.

She grabbed her purse from the bench, bookmarked her paperback and hid it away. "You're presenting on randomness and subatomic particles, is that right?"

"Yes," he said, and quoted the title, "'The Unpredictable Microcosm.' But I've kept it very basic, for general assembly."

"Of course," she said. "A survey for the layperson."

"Something like that," he said. On the other side of the tennis courts was the sprawling green, and here there were always students hanging out, studying, filling the benches, lying on blankets looking at the clouds. Rachel remained attached to his side. She engaged in light conversation, about her life, her studies. She was twenty-eight and enjoyed her Von Neumann Algebra class but was struggling mightily with Analyses in Non-Euclidean Space. "Difficult for anyone," he said kindly, privately thinking the course was a waste of time. He idly recommended something in special relativity but she shrugged it off; she enjoyed playing with numbers, not manipulating reality, she said.

When they arrived at the lecture hall there was already a small crowd gathered, though there was still a half hour before Rick's presentation. Rachel followed him past the gathering in the lobby down a long hall that led to a small green room. He said, "I was hoping to spend a few minutes warming up."

"Of course," she said, but she followed him into the room.

He said, hoping she would take the hint, "Perhaps I'll see you after the presentation?"

"Oh, I'm not going to stay for that," she said. "But you can tell me about it later." She paused. "If I see you again." It did not seem to be a question. She offered him her hand, as before, and again he took it, held it for a moment. Then she darted out the door. An odd girl, he thought, and a bit pushy. He had been too kind to her.

A very long time before this – in the beginning, as it were – Adam, the first created man, called his son Seth to his side.

"I am soon to die," he said. Seth bowed his head, wanting to object, but he knew it to be true. His father was nine-hundred-and-thirty years old and had been ill for some time. Adam put a hand on his shoulder and looked at him intently. "Within you is the best of your mother and myself. I believe you have always been favored by the Lord – more than anyone not born of Eden." He sighed heavily. Seth came down to his knees next to Adam, so their eyes were on the same level. "Last night, the Lord came to me in a dream," Adam said.

Seth's eyes were wide. He had never spoken with the Lord. "What did he say, Father?"

For the first time, Adam smiled. "He said there will be a *new* Garden, for you and your children."

Seth, having never seen Eden, could only imagine its wonder.

"But first, there is something you must do," Adam said. "You must go to Eden, where the Guardian stands with a flaming sword. Speak my name, and tell him that you are my son. The Lord has commanded him to let you pass."

"I do not know the way," said Seth.

"I will tell you how to find it. Listen: when you have entered, you will need to find the Tree of Life. But you must eat none of its fruit! That fruit isn't meant for us, but for the children of our children. Instead, you must take three seeds from the tree and bring them back to me."

"I will do it, father," said Seth, though he didn't understand how his father could know these things. He didn't doubt them; Doubt was still a newborn babe, and had not yet been baptized in the waters of the earth.

Adam smiled gently. "I know that you will. If I am dead when you return," —Seth looked about to object, but Adam waved a hand to silence him— "then before you return me to dust, you must place the seeds in my mouth."

"I understand," Seth said, though he didn't. Still, he immediately went to do as his father had asked him.

Meanwhile, in the present, Will watched his friend Richard Mayliss come to the close of a dry and – Will thought – disappointing lecture. The swirling animation on the screen behind him was a dangerous distraction. Rick himself even seemed distracted, Will decided, delivering the string of words with none of his usual enthusiasm for the content they contained.

"Thus the Synchronic Effect, as I have called it," Rick was saying, "is supported by some measured quantum behavior, though still nothing that would definitively prove its existence. As we now know, all systems co-exist as superimposed wave functions until disturbed by an outside observer. This is no longer thought to apply only to subatomic particles; that is, this ambiguous nature seems to apply to all reality regardless of size." From his tone, he may as well have been describing the effects of gravity.

"There is some debate within our own team concerning the nature of the effect. Dr. Evians is of the opinion that as-yet undiscovered particles, which he has dubbed *synchrons*, interact with observed wave functions at the moment of collapse. I myself favor the idea that this synchronicity is a product of the interaction between already known subatomic particles, and that further study of quantum probability will reveal a synchronic effect to be inherent to that interaction. Indeed, I expect this effect to apply to the interaction of all systems.

"My own determination is that these systems are able to maintain superposition, despite collapse, if regular pulses are applied to the environment, keeping some awareness of other possible states."

Here, Will sat forward, thinking, *He's talking about the Artifact.* It was the word "pulses" that drew his attention. Rick had brought up these pulses several times over the last several weeks, as he'd opened up more and more about the Artifact.

But as Rick continued, Will shook his head, sinking back into the seat. He wasn't a scientist, and he could barely follow most of what Rick was saying.

"This has been demonstrated repeatedly at the subatomic level, here in our laboratory. We hope to soon show the same result with individual atoms and molecules," Rick concluded. "Are there any questions?"

There were none. Will watched the woman in front of him stifle a yawn as she stood. He waited for Rick, smirking at him when he came close. But the professor was pulled aside by an inquisitive student, so Will went out to wait for him in the lobby. He stopped near two students when he overheard them talking.

"...whether it makes sense or not, I don't know. I just feel like he's leaving things out." This was a short, skinny youth who looked like he should still be in a high school. His partner was tall and lanky with a splash of red hair that came down to his shoulders.

"Maybe he's an intuitive thinker," that one remarked. "What was with the Eye of Ra? Why do you think he picked that?"

"That's one of the things I'm talking about," the short one said. "Why all the quasi-historical mumbo-jumbo? What does ancient Egyptian philosophy have to do with modern physics?"

"I think he was trying to relate it to the idea of synchronicity somehow," said the tall one.

"Obviously. He called it a 'synchronic effect,' it's like a blatant rip-off. But I don't think he *really* understands what synchronicity is." As the two wandered away, Will heard the second youth mumble, "Still, he's brilliant, isn't he?"

15

Will suppressed a twinge of jealousy – *Humility is the solid foundation of all virtues*, he reminded himself, and when Rick came out of the auditorium, finally free of his gaggle of admirers, Will greeted him with a smile.

"Nice, with the glasses," he said.

Rick flashed a quick smile before returning to his former nerd-face. "Had trouble with my contacts," he said. "They were making my eyes water."

"I didn't catch the whole thing," said Will, "just the second half."

"I saw you come in," said Rick.

"Yeah," said Will. "Anyway, it's mostly over my head." Rick kept his silence. Will went on, "I overheard some kids talking about synchronicity."

Rick raised any eyebrow, but then it fell again, in quick dismissal. "I mentioned it several times," he said. "The idea bothered them? They just can't correlate my technical definition with what they read in their astrology magazines. That's why I've tried to use a more precise name, to separate it from an old, uselessly ambiguous concept."

"That explains it," Will said.

"Explains what?"

Will shrugged. "They just thought you seemed confused about it."

Rick frowned. He said nothing more, but Will, knowing Rick, thought he'd be dwelling on the criticism the rest of the day.

They went together to admire the Artifact. It was Rick's treasure, an eons old reminder of the unknown, but an Eye as well, into that unknown. Its glow was more golden than the precious molten metal it was formed from. It seemed solid, impenetrable to understanding, and the carvings of the back told of its ancient Egyptian origin, but nothing more. Two figures stood on either side of an empty throne, one male, one female. The male looked toward the throne, the female away, so that as far as the wearer of the helmet was concerned, they both looked towards the right.

Rick had studied the drawings endlessly, but their lines were clean and simple, devoid of any adorning symbol. He had searched through time and space for their meaning, but they were nowhere duplicated. The hieroglyphs underneath, however, were easy to translate:

"The Eye of Set."

To Rick, it also appeared possible that the complex carving of the god "Set" underneath the inscription had replaced an earlier carving. A marking above the head of the figure looked like it could have been a solar disc partially removed, and he thought the head might have been altered – maybe before it had been a falcon, reworked into the Set animal.

It was his own suspicion that the earlier engraving had read either "Horus" or possibly "Ra," as the only image on the front of the helmet was clearly the Eye of Horus. He didn't know why it had been changed (or how, for that matter – his own experimentations on the gold surface had revealed it to be impervious to damage).

He had been in possession of the Artifact for a long time, and still knew almost nothing of its origin.

Rick looked at Will, thinking, *I shouldn't have shown it to him.* For sixteen years, he hadn't told anyone. Now he knew the secret was in danger; best friend – only *trusted* friend – or not, Will was bursting with so much hidden knowledge it was spilling over into his eyebrows like popcorn. "Relax, all right?" he told him, and immediately recognized when Will took offense.

But Will apologized, as was his way. "I can't help it. I don't know how you keep it so locked up like that." He shook his head. "I guess over time you get used to it."

"Time does put some perspective on things," Rick said.

"You don't ever worry about saying too much?" Will asked.

"What do you mean?"

"Like, that they'll figure it out from your presentation."

18

"Some things will be worked out," Rick said. "That's kind of the point." He lifted the Artifact out of its protected case. It thrummed – the hum the result of a rapid cyclic pulse, Rick believed – and they both were silent, each feeling its energy pervade the room, raising their heart rate and their body temperature.

"But they won't figure *this* out," said Will.

"How could they?" said Rick. Then, almost a whisper: "*I* still haven't figured it out."

"You've been doing this a long time," Will commented. "Let me ask you..." His voice had an apologetic quality even before he spoke the words: "This is the first time this has occurred to me. Your whole history, I mean, all the work you've done... the papers and everything... the experiments... You didn't really come up with any of that, did you?"

Rick looked at him sharply. "Those are my discoveries," he said immediately. "I discovered those things."

"Well, you learned them from the artifact." Will tried not to emphasize the word, give it special weight, the way it was capitalized in his head.

"I discovered those things," Rick repeated. "I pieced them together, myself."

"I'm not saying anything bad about it," Will said. "Just asking. Is there anything you came up with *without* the helmet?"

"Those are my discoveries," said Rick. "Those are *my* formulae on those papers that *I* worked out, *myself.* Those are *my* conclusions. You think I'm *stealing?*"

"No, I didn't say that."

"That's my math in those papers," Rick insisted. "That's *my* math. Those are *my* experiments."

"I know!" said Will. "Sorry!" He grinned. "It's a good thing you've got going, though."

Rick glanced over, saw his expression, grinned with him. "I know," he said. "It's like God has given me a gift."

"You don't believe in God," Will pointed out, and Rick shrugged. After a moment, Will asked, "Are you going to let me ride it again?"

Rick thought the word "ride" a strange choice, like the artifact was a motorcycle or an attraction at an amusement park. They stood over it, Rick on the south, Will on the east, and out at Rick's cabin it was likely there wasn't another soul for miles.

"I don't know," Rick said. "Things can be dangerous for a beginner."

"You said that before," said Will.

"There's a lot the Artifact can do," Rick said. He set the helmet gently on the table. "Manipulating the synchronic field can have unpredictable consequences, some of which could be drastic."

"Is that what it does?" asked Will. "Affect the

20

synchronic field?" He had an inquisitive, studious look on his face that Rick found embarrassing, a desperate plea for acceptance into the intellectual assembly.

"It probably does much more than that," he said. And even if I explained it to you in detail, he thought, showed you the computations, you still could never understand what it is capable of.

"Well, you're the genius," Will said, echoing Rick's thoughts. Then he said, "It seems louder than usual, today."

"Does it?" Rick said. He thought so as well. These emanations it put off, this cyclical hum – it created fields that had become the focus of Rick's study. He heard it always; it had grown louder over the years, but he grew less aware of it, and now the sound was like his own breathing, or heartbeat – an unnoticeable part of himself.

He found himself enjoying Will's excitement, thinking – as he had more and more over the years – maybe it was time to let the secret out, at least a little bit. Maybe the time had come to share the Artifact with the world.

He told Will graciously, "Sure, I'll let you use it again. But you have to be careful. Look before you leap. Don't be too aggressive." He picked it up and set it into Will's hands, who cradled it as though he were about to baptize a newborn.

Will couldn't take his eyes off of it. "It's heavy," he said. "I forgot."

"You don't feel it so much when you're wearing it," Rick said, also looking at the helmet, stifling the feeling of animal jealousy that stirred in his gut.

"Yeah," Will said. He couldn't stop grinning. He took a deep breath and slid the Artifact over his head.

Dr. Henry Evians was a little disappointed in how little Rick Mayliss had talked about synchrons and as he walked across campus from the auditorium back to his office in Wright Hall, he decided he would have to develop his own speech, scheduled for next month, around that very topic. He was not really surprised Mayliss had skirted the idea. Richard had admitted he had a hard time accepting the idea of the little things. But they *have* to exist, though Evians. Nothing else could explain the huge variations they'd observed in the Effect.

Indeed, according to Evians' math and the results of the particle accelerator simulations, there had to exist at *least* 3 different types of synchronic particles.

He had already named them: the significator, the archon, and the homogenort. Harmonious words, he felt, that would sound good in the presentation.

He unlocked his office, powered up his computer,

and logged on to the server running the simulation software. A few simulations were listed in the active workspace already, but none were his; he ignored them and instead opened the settings dialogue for a new one.

He hesitated before defining the initial variables – it was mostly guesswork at this point – but finally he typed in some parameters and clicked GENERATE. *Preparing...* the screen declared. *Est. 3 min.*

Three minutes, he thought. The coffee pot was on the windowsill, half full of cold coffee. He flipped it on and let it start to heat, then opened the window, the sound of singing birds and the breath of cool campus air transforming the stale office. The green outside was empty and silent, the sky starting to turn dark. He hardly noticed as he poured lukewarm coffee into his mug and sat down at the simulator.

The computer dinged; the particle was prepared. All right, thought Evians, pulling a notepad and a calculator from the pile on his desk, let's put this archon through some paces.

It stormed sorrowfully that night, and Rick pondered – as he babysat Will, silently riding the Artifact – how deceptive could be the atmosphere, how out of sync could be the weather, how life was no movie where the mood was prepared and controlled by the subtlest of manipulations, but how in real life the sky could weep, the earth could grieve, while he and Will could exult at the peak of their lives and careers, everything moving to its own rhythm, singing its own song, slave to no script or storyboard or director.

He thought these long thoughts as the time unwound slowly, Will unmoving save for the occasional adjustment of an eyepiece. Rick had no way to know what he saw or experienced. Will did not speak; Rick did not know if that meant he had no conversations. The body on this side would not – could not – replicate its experience from within the Artifact.

He should have warned Will to be careful – *most* careful – in his activity. Had he cautioned him enough? He watched Will twist the left eyepiece with trepidation. The turning of that knob caused reality to slip out of sync with time.

Time. The mystery of time was one of the greatest mysteries of the Artifact. There was no way to know how much of it passed for Will. There was no correlation between the long seconds here and whatever stream it was that Will chose to experience.

He had no idea how it was possible. It was a technology sufficiently advanced to be called magic, but Rick knew it *was* technology. He would unravel its mysteries eventually. He watched as the very next moment (always the very next moment after the turning of the left eyepiece) Will ripped the helmet away, gasping, his breath coming suddenly in short, hard coughs. Rick waited until he had recovered.

"The Shadow," Will explained.

Rick had already come to that conclusion. The Shadow always came eventually. If it didn't, one could get lost in the Artifact forever.

Evians was going over simulation results when his watch began beeping at him. It was a high-tech Seiko deal his daughter had gotten him, with about fifteen buttons on the green face. It was huge and dominated his arm. He constantly felt a vague embarrassment about it – when he noticed it – but he had to admit it was an amazingly useful little device, with a high resolution display, a calculator, the afore-mentioned alarm, internet functionality, you name it.

He looked at the digital display and was shocked at the time. *7:30am*, it blinked, and beneath that it said: *REMINDER: mtng gary 8:00.*

Worked through the night again, thought Evians, guiltily. Forgot to call Kristen, his sixteen year old daughter, tell her he'd be late. He sighed. Still, she would understand. She wouldn't worry about him any more than usual.

He poured himself another cup of coffee and rubbed his eyes, feeling the exhaustion now that he'd been snapped out of his work trance. He had no classes that day, which was good. Usually he tried to maintain office hours throughout the day, to make himself available to students, but he thought after meeting with Gary he might need to take the rest of the morning off and catch a nap.

He straightened his desk and propped the office door open. A couple students walked by while he was standing there. He recognized one from one of his classes a year or so ago. He couldn't remember her name. She gave him a pretty smile, said, "Morning, Dr. Evians."

"Morning," he said, and watched them head down to the end of the hall and disappear up the stairs.

He sat back down at his desk and dialed his daughter on the phone. "Hey, pumpkin," he said when she picked up on the other end.

"Hi, Daddy," she said, sounding much fresher than he felt. "I'm getting ready for school."

"Me too," he said.

"Did you sleep in the office again?" she said, and he heard her smile in her voice.

"Didn't sleep."

"Aww, Dad," she said, but she didn't sound recriminating, she never did. "I did the dishes and the trash," she said, matter-of-factly, "and I left some of the chili with beans in the fridge."

"Sounds good," he said.

"It's too spicy," she apologized. "Oh, I also recorded Brainiac for you. It was a good one. You coming home tonight?"

"I hope so," he said. He waved Gary inside, who had shown up early and was patiently waiting outside the office.

"Don't forget I have band tonight," Kristen said, "if you come home early and I'm not there."

"I won't," he said. "Love you, pumpkin."

"You too, Daddy," she said, and hung up.

"My daughter," he said to Gary, not bothering to mask the pride that always crept into his voice when he talked about her.

"Is that her?" asked Gary, looking at a framed picture on the bookshelf. In it, she had short hair and a huge smile that was mostly braces, her face still round with baby fat.

"Yes, that's an old one, four or five years now." He added, "That's her mother with her," then, regretfully, "who's no longer with us."

"I'm sorry," said Gary.

Evians never knew how to reply to that, so instead he said, "I saw you at Dr. Mayliss's presentation last night. What did you think?"

27

"He's impressive," said Gary.

"He is," Evians agreed, "he certainly is." Then, "So your paper. Have you thought about it?"

"I have," said Gary, then in a rush, "and I know you might not approve the topic, I know it's a stretch." Evians raised his eyebrows, giving no sign of encouragement. Gary cleared his throat. "I want to, if possible, explore the possibility of altering a particle's vector in the fourth dimension."

Evians frowned, then chuckled. "Time travel," he said. "Very speculative."

"Well, yes," said Gary.

"You realize this paper is worth half your grade for this term?"

"Yes, sir," said Gary.

"And you realize it must be an *original* solution," said Evians sternly. "Not one of the Thorne variations or some such."

"Of course," said Gary.

Evians raised his eyebrows. "You have already developed a solution?"

"Not yet," said Gary, "but I'm working on it."

Evians smile was ever-so-slightly condescending. "A lot of people are."

"I think I may be close," Gary said, "or at least, I'm getting some good indicators in the simulations. I've based it around two papers. One is yours, the other is by Dr. Mayliss."

This aroused Evians' curiosity. "Really?" He leaned forward. "Which papers?"

"The first one is your paper on the attractive force of synchrons," Gary said.

"Hmmmm," murmured Evians, thinking back on it. "Of course, synchrons remain theoretical."

"Yes," said Gary. "The second is Dr. Mayliss' paper on 'Spin and State Transference in Boson Particles.' Do you know it?"

Evians' brow furrowed in thought. "I do seem to remember reading something like that. It's a few years past now, yes?"

Gary nodded.

"It didn't make much of a splash," said Evians. But as the details of the paper came back to him, it started his mind churning. "The attractive force of synchrons," he said aloud, "and spin and state transference in quark-like particles." He plucked a pen out of his holder and started tapping it on his desk, unaware of the activity, his eyes roaming without seeing as he began putting the two papers together in his head. Gary watched him think, not saying anything. Eventually, Evians' eyes refocused. "Interesting," he said. "I may have a glimmer of what you're trying to get at." He had lost all traces of condescension. "But it's still very speculative."

"Yes," Gary agreed. "That's why I wanted to talk to you in person."

"I'll allow it," said Evians. "But I won't cut any slack on your work. *Hard numbers*, that's what I grade on. Choose time travel at your own risk."

"Yes, sir," said Gary. "Thank you!"

Evians watched the student scramble away, but his mind had already turned back to the two papers, mentally juxtaposing them. The student, Gary, was a bright kid. He might have stumbled onto something.

Let me run a simulation, he thought, and turned to his computer. He took a sip of his coffee, then frowned into the cold cup. He clicked the icon for the simulator. While it was loading, he walked over to the coffee pot and poured what remained, steaming, into his mug.

Have to make some more coffee, he thought. I'll do that after I start the simulation. He sat back down and started entering variables.

Rabalyov's Last Concerto wept with cold metal strings, mourned with the ghost of its lost creator, possessed of his spirit in clef and stave, animated in fingers that stroked ivory tendrils that connected the living to the dead. The strings danced a tragic inspiration a century old, and now Will, re-awakened, could feel himself drawn inexorably through the pain of a long-forgotten wound. How had he forgotten, he wondered, the sacred voodoo of *this* artifact, this instrument of passage, a vessel for souls to make a brief and amorphous return.

He stopped playing, overwhelmed with emotion and feeling foolish for it, thinking about the previous night. Will, a music director at Forrest Park Methodist Church, had worn the Artifact with the intention of viewing – merely viewing – the invention of the piano. An idle curiosity. Instead, he had come upon an ancient Greek minstrel with an obsession for strings and sound, and not knowing why – except it felt like he was supposed to – Will had gone from viewing to visiting and talked with the strange fat man for hours.

He had not told Rick; he knew he would be furious. Will had – without meaning to – told the minstrel about the piano, which wouldn't be invented for another two millennium.

It was the gleam in the minstrel's eye that had alerted him to his mistake. *Could* an obsessive musician before the birth of Christ reconstruct Will's vague description of the advanced instrument? Might he have changed history?

If so, he thought, it only seemed to be reflected in his own renewed appreciation for the piano's artistic potential. He had played Rabalyov many times before. This was the first time he had so deeply realized the inherent magic he was performing.

He tried to compose himself as he walked away from the grand piano, carried the book back into the rehearsal room, and prepared for the arrival of his choir members.

Having something to hide was a new experience for Will, and he wasn't sure he liked what it was doing to him. On the one hand, knowledge of the Artifact filled him with an exhilaration, an exultation unlike anything in his past, but on the other, he could feel a separation he had never felt. More and more he was coming to see the world he lived in as shallow and uninteresting. He was afraid he was losing his passion for his work, losing interest in the people around him.

Louis and Mary arrived together, talking in loud tones about the play they had attended over the weekend. They were good people, but today Will had to force a smile to his face.

"Did you hear about Kassie?" Mary asked him, giving him a hug.

"Yes," he said, "she called this morning."

"Poor thing," Mary said sympathetically. Kassie suffered from fibromyalgia, some days much worse than others. It had been a particularly trying week.

"Of course I told her not to come," Will said. "You and Lynne have got the alto covered for this Sunday."

"George isn't going to make it either," interjected

Louis, sounding worried, as that meant he would likely be the only bass. Louis had a magnificent voice that was well-hidden by his fear of using it. It would occasionally come out in rehearsal and everyone would look momentarily startled, then when Louis realized they were actually paying attention it would disappear again as his shoulders collapsed and his stomach sunk back to its usual nervous condition.

"I can sing with your part," Will reassured him. "Just pay attention to me while I conduct." Mary had started arranging chairs in an arc – which Will had forgotten to do. "Let me help you with that," he said.

As they finished the rest of the choir arrived. They were so *loud*, thought Will, the incessant chatter far more irritating than usual. He took a deep breath, tapped a pencil on the music stand. "Let's get warmed up." It took another minute or so for everyone to settle down. Still no sign of Katya, the piano player.

Will stepped over to the piano and played a scale. They all sang along. How could they be singing together, Will thought, and still seem so apart? Lynne, with her stiff dyed hair and bright makeup, sat upright, singing out, her eyebrows raised, but her eyes lost in the church bulletin, no real interest in the exercises. They were all like that, in their own world, not taking it seriously, just warming up.

It's just scales, he reminded himself. His irritation

was unwarranted, and he realized it. It was not their fault; they were too saturated, inundated with these harmonies in all the most mundane moments – grocery shopping, watch-ing TV, stuck in traffic, in the office, in the nursery, in the elevator; wasted on them from their very birth.

At that moment Katya arrived, hurried and out of breath, apologizing in her thick Russian accent, her eyes sad and stressed, and Will hated himself for thinking ill of her only moments before.

"I had to come from Rockstone," she said, as she always did. She taught private lessons on the other side of town, and the traffic was terrible every Wednesday.

He looked into her sad, stressed eyes and felt himself divide, quake apart like an island broken upon a fault, the larger part visible in his eyes, his voice, sympathetic and patient, the smaller part hidden but insistent, growing in urgency. Quit crying! this part wanted to tell Katya. You're wallowing in self-pity! Your unhappiness is your own fault, this part wanted to say. But the other part would never let it.

He felt himself divide. But he breathed deeply, and while Katya opened her binder on the piano, he pulled himself back together.

When Rick left his office the next day, the girl – Rachel – was there. It seemed she had been waiting on him, but of this he couldn't be sure. She said to him, like she had been thinking about it, "What is it about my name?"

"What do you mean?" he said.

"Don't be stiff," she said, "I saw how you reacted."

He took affront to her description – stiff – but still, he answered her question. "I knew a girl with that name, a long time ago."

"Loved, you mean," she said, in a way that would accept no argument.

He frowned at her, trying to let her know she was bothering him. But when she just kept looking back, expressionless, he finally said, "Yes, loved."

"Was it very long ago?" When he didn't answer right away, she went on, "It must have been. You can always tell when someone's been wearing their sadness a long time. It's like they're resigned to it, like they've accepted they had their happiness once, and now it's in the past. I wish I could say I feel for you, but I can't imagine that. You're not that old, you know. How do you know you've even lived half of your life? If you loved once, you can love again."

She was a strange young woman, he thought, not sure if she was coming on to him or if she was just the type to butt into other people's lives. He said, "Do you even realize you're being rude?" and she *hmmphed* like that was a foolish thing to say. He said, "I suppose in your generation" – she frowned at that – "it's permissible to speak your mind freely, but when I was growing up, we were taught manners."

"I have manners," she said.

"Loss is a sensitive subject."

"For sensitive people," she shrugged. "Are you one of those?"

"No," he said shortly. He walked past her, but she followed. Now he was certain she had been waiting for him. Great, he thought, I have a student stalker. "I really have to get home," he said.

"Why?" she said. "You just told me you don't have anyone waiting for you, right?"

"A man can have a very fulfilling life," Rick said, "without there being any romance in it."

She laughed. Then she thought about it, and laughed again. "Of course he can," she said. Then, with the air of one who was used to being easily forgiven, "I don't mean to be rude."

"I imagine most rude people don't," he said.

Something in her eyes just then made him feel immediately bad about his tone, but it was too late. She offered him her hand abruptly, and when he took it there was a resistance that hadn't been there before, a wounded rigidity that seemed unlike what little he knew of her. "Well, it was fine conversing with you again, Dr. Mayliss," she said. "Adieu."

She walked away without waiting for a response. She left him disturbed, irritated. Was he angry? He couldn't be sure.

It was the name, he thought, Rachel. It was a name meant to cause him turmoil.

One, two, four, eight, sixteen years. Longer, thanks to the Artifact, and while it was true he had worn his grief like a cloak, he had thought it hidden from the casual eye. He grew older, time flew more swiftly, but his memories of Rachel, brief as they were, were as clear and close as ever. He had loved her. He still loved her, but he hated her memory with equal passion.

The first year, he blamed her for her death; this was easy to do, she had committed suicide.

The second year, the blame continued; no, it got worse. It festered. He thought her suicide was selfish. An act of weakness. When they had first met he had thought she was strong. He had been attracted to her strength. He had been so disappointed. So *hurt*, so disappointed. He had not understood. He still didn't understand.

Rachel, Rachel. She had come back to haunt him, a

strange doppelganger meant to torment him. A ghost from a past he had turned his back on.

Four years of guilt, of wondering, was it *me*? What had *I* done? Eight years searching, frustrated, the Shadow a specter at every turn.

Sixteen years with the Artifact. Sixteen years, he should be over her.

Sixteen years. By now, he should have healed.

Sixteen years ago, as an undergraduate physics student at Stanford, Rick had met an archaeology major named Rachel on a university-sponsored rock climbing expedition. They were both very similar people; hard workers, detached but passionate intellectuals, competitive, comfortably entrenched in different fields – he in physics, she in archaeology.

They soon were talking about marriage – planning, really, as fit both their natures – but then Rachel was accepted for an internship halfway around the world – a dig in Patara, Turkey. While she was gone something changed. They exchanged letters and phone calls, but as time went on she became more and more distant. He tried to ask her about it, but she brushed it aside – it was nothing.

But she was slipping away from him and he knew it. Maybe she was seeing someone else, maybe it was her experiences in Turkey that had changed her. He just didn't know.

After her return from the six month program they talked about their future. Her plans, she said, had not changed. "I love you," she said, "I'll always love you," but there had been something in her eyes that remained dark and closed, something in her voice that had become empty. Three weeks later he was at the university when he got a call from her father. She had cut her arms and legs and bled to death in the bathtub.

"Why?" he had asked, as everything inside him started to shrivel.

"You don't know?" her dad had asked, sounding accusing to Rick at first, but then Rick could hear he was crying as he said, "We were hoping you would know something." He mumbled something unintelligible, then, "She never said anything to us."

Rick didn't know how to respond.

"Anyway," her father said, after an awkward moment, "she left boxes for you at the apartment. They've got your name on them. She was..." – his voice broke – "very prepared."

She always was, thought Rick.

"You still have a key?" her father asked.

"Yes," he said.

"You can go get them Friday, if that's okay. After the

funeral."

"Okay," Rick said dully.

"Rick?" her dad said. "I'm so sorry."

"Me, too," he said. Then, unpracticed words squeezed out by anguish: "I love you, Dad."

The quiet man sounded surprised but gratified. "We love you too, son." But they had not remained close as the years passed.

The Saturday after her death he went to her apartment. It had been completely emptied expect for five boxes in the middle of the dining room floor. "Rick" was written in black marker on each one, in Rachel's handwriting. They were taped shut, neatly stacked. He looked at the precise letters, straight and even, each exactly the same height and width, like she had traced them from a stencil. Her writing always looked like that – tiny, narrowly scrunched together, but clean, careful, and precise.

The same handwriting filled pages of letters in a box by his bed. He had been poring over them for days, obsessed, looking for a clue. She had never given any indication of depression, self-destructive tendencies, any desire to end her own life. Whatever she had dealt with she had concealed behind the distance that had slowly grown, the façade that had become colder and colder over time.

He stood in the bathroom for minutes that

disappeared into eternity, staring into the bathtub. Everything was clean and sterile. The shower curtain had been removed. The bathtub looked extra-white, bleached.

He packed the boxes into his car and drove off. He almost hit a parked car and realized how unsettled he was, so he pulled over and turned off the engine. His body trembled like a leaf in fear of storm. Then he cried violently, sobs wrenched painfully from his chest. Some pathetic voice in his head tried to offer comfort. *It's okay to cry*, it said. But he answered himself out loud, sounding like a child to his own ears, "No, it's not, it's not okay." This was a chorus, a refrain he bawled over and over again.

When the sobs came less and less, separated by longer and longer silences, he became aware of a sound, a steady humming. It had been going for a while, he realized, but consumed by grief he hadn't noticed it. It sounded like it was coming from one of the boxes in the back seat.

He got out of the car, opened the back door, and separated the box from the rest, setting it in the street next to the curb. He put his ear close, but couldn't identify it. Just a steady, soft hum.

He used his car keys to slit the tape and opened the box. Inside was another box – a case with a latch, the interior lined with thick cloth. It contained a golden helmet – an artifact.

He lifted it out of the box. It was heavier than it appeared. He had never seen anything like it, but he immediately took it to be of Egyptian design; it reminded him most of the pharaoh masks worn by mummies. The eyes were unusual; the outsides of the eyes were marked, joined by a symbol of the Eye of Horus in the center of the forehead. Its most unusual aspect was the shape of the eyes – each protruded outwards, creating cylinders that gave the vague impression of binoculars.

The hum seemed to be coming from the eyes, and has he held it in front of him, the air seemed to shimmer, like heat was rising from the metal. He put his hand near one of the eye-cylinders and felt nothing. No heat. No vibrations when he touched it, tapped it. Grasped it, putting his hand around the entire cylinder.

It was neither hot nor cold.

Finally, he put the helmet on his head. This was its obvious intention. At first it was dark, then he straightened it and his eyes found the eyeholes. As light streamed in, the weight of the helmet seemed to disappear. Sound was muted; everything seemed distant and masked by a gentle whooshing sound, like air circulating.

Through the eyeholes he could see the interior of the

car, through the window he was facing. The right eye was crystal clear. The left eye was blurred, out of focus. He realized then why the eyes were cylinders: he was looking through lenses, like binoculars. He reached up and grabbed the left eye where it protruded, and it turned easily, gradually coming into focus with the other.

When it did, he felt suddenly nauseated, his stomach cramping, his gut wrenching like before, sobbing in the car, and he was gripped by a cold chill that carried grief and thoughts of Rachel. A car passed, and he saw the driver looking at him curiously. He wondered what strange figure he made, his polo shirt topped by this piece of Egyptian magnificence. I should put it away, he thought, and he started to take it off.

And that was when he saw Rachel, looking at him through the back window. There was no doubt it was her, standing in the street behind the car. Wrinkling her nose at him. Saying something he couldn't hear.

"What?" he said, or shouted. His voice echoed with a terrible thunder within the helmet, but he hardly noticed, unable to take his eyes off Rachel, her image saturated with color, the artifact's lenses bathing her with a preternatural glow.

She's alive, was the only thought he could achieve. He started toward her, but lost sight of her when he turned his head, and when he looked back, she was gone.

"Rachel?" he said, his whisper reverberating as though in a deep cavern. He went behind the car, to where she had been standing.

Nothing.

Seeing things, he thought. He noticed a group of kids ogling him from the stairwell of the apartments by the street. Staring at the helmet, he realized. Feeling foolish, he climbed into the back seat of the car, pushing the boxes over to make room, and took the helmet off.

For a strange moment, it seemed to suck at his head, like air into a vacuum. Then it came off and everything suddenly seemed normal again. His mental state had changed with the helmet on, he realized. It had done something to his mind.

He thought of the image of Rachel – so clear and real – and felt a chill.

A hallucination, he thought.

He packed the helmet carefully back into its box and drove home, the back seat humming ominously the entire way.

The phone rang. Gary picked it up.

"Hey, roomie," said Ben – Gary rolled his eyes at the secret code word – "what are you up to?"

The code word "roomie" meant Ben was bringing a girl back to the room and would want some privacy. He sighed heavily, then said, "I was just about to head to the computer lab to study."

So he stuffed the books he was working from into his bag and started the twenty-minute walk to the campus. He liked to walk, to get a breath of fresh air, clear his head.

He had been working on the time travel project, of course. He couldn't get it out of his mind. He had imagined a visualization – a spontaneous intuition – of how the synchrons, if they existed, would behave. It was like smoke rings intersecting, was the best he could describe it, but the metaphor didn't do it justice. It had been more than visual... He had felt the interaction kinesthetically, like juggling. He could still call it to mind, but the clarity of the initial vision was fading.

He had read the two papers one after the other, over and over, notebook in front of him. He was sure of the reality of synchrons – never mind that two of the greatest minds in physics still argued over their existence. Brilliant as he thought Mayliss was, Gary agreed with Dr. Evians: in the end, some kind of particle, some kind of unit, had to be responsible for the fields that Mayliss had discovered. It was obvious, he thought, frustrated, once you've *seen* it.

Out on the campus green, he had to stop and sit on a bench, focusing on his thoughts. He had almost seen a solution. He had envisioned, for a moment, a synchronic wormhole, a gravity void created by the intersecting fields. But it's *not* a vortex, he thought. It's a particle.

No revelation came. He got up and walked again, disappointed. There was still so much he needed to know. The library was closed at this time of night, but he could hop on the internet at the computer lab and do some research. If he was in luck, the simulation queue would be light, and he might be able to start a process.

After rehearsal, Pastor Drew – whose wife Lynne was in the choir – pulled Will aside, handing him a DVD. "Can we go over the movie clip for Sunday?"

"Sure," said Will, making some final notations in his score, "give me just one second." He took the DVD – something called *Tuesday Night Movie Theater* that he'd never seen – and popped it into the player on his computer. After a moment, the DVD menu came up on his monitor. He scrolled down to where it said *Scene Selections* and hit 'enter.'

"I think it's scene six," said Pastor Drew.

Will chose scene six, and they watched a few seconds

as a couple argued while seated in a movie theater. "I think this is it," said Pastor Drew, but a second or two later the guy in the scene dropped the F-bomb and Pastor Drew winced. "Go forward a little," he said, so Will hit the fast-forward button and waited. "Here it is, I think," said Pastor Drew, so Will hit play again. Now the couple was standing up and leaving the theater. "Yes," said Drew, "it starts here."

They watched for a bit as the man and woman argued about the existence of God.

"And end right there," said Pastor Drew. "That's all I want. It's for the end of the sermon. I have the notes here. Should I give them to you? I've e-mailed a copy to Dave." His face was bright with earnest perspiration, his forehead crinkled like a sheet of notepaper crumpled and opened a thousand times, like a scribbled confession that refused to remain discarded.

"Sure," said Will, taking the notes, but, he felt, little of the burden.

"See this highlight?" Drew said. "About the incomprehensibility of God? See here, a God of love and wrath? Punishment and reward? Compassionate yet cold?"

"I see," said Will. "I'll run it over to Dave."

"Thank you, Will. Have him call me if he needs anything."

"Of course," said Will.

On the way home, inching through traffic, Pastor Drew turned the radio off and in the resulting silence tapped his worries out on the steering wheel with his left index finger.

"He didn't get it," he said to the empty car.

He was thinking of Will.

It was the punishment and reward angle Will didn't like, Drew could see that. Will took that to mean capricious, arbitrary, and Will wouldn't be able to accept such a God. Will was – like so many modern Christians, Drew thought – sterilized by some watered-down, Romanized version of a benevolent father figure whose dominant traits were compassion and pride for his divine son.

Which was, of course, the same God Drew himself had been raised to worship. The same God that had driven his early passion for the risen Savior. And it was true, God was capable of these traits. But there was a deeper Truth, Drew had come to understand, a Truth that was a bit harder to swallow. A more mature Truth, is how Drew thought of it, instead of the simple Truth meant for children: He loves you, all your sins are forgiven through the compassionate Savior. But for adults, a deeper Truth, by which they would be weighed and measured: I have given you charge of my domain, and will judge your investments upon My return.

Drew shook his head, contemplating his sermon, thinking, it wasn't only Will who wouldn't get it. No matter how many times he delivered it, it still remained his most difficult – and least popular – message:

The faith of Abraham is not found among his children, who do not know how to listen to the Son. The shepherd appeared, but the sheep fail to follow.

"I don't get it," said Dave, watching the clip with Will. They were at Dave's home computer, Will standing just behind Dave's wheelchair. "What's the sermon about?" Dave was a volunteer at the church, who did video editing and other technical tasks from time to time.

Will consulted his notepad. "I've got, 'God's incomprehensible, love/wrath, punishment/re-ward, compassion/coldness."

Dave's eyebrows contorted. "Okay," he said doubtfully. "Shouldn't be a problem."

"Ours is not to understand," said Will, "just to edit the video."

"Right," said Dave. "It'll take one blank DVD. Consider it a donation."

"The Lord appreciates your generosity," said Will. He was admiring the gadgets strewn around Dave's office.

"What's this?"

Dave wheeled over to see what Will was looking at. "Capture device," he said. "Multi-format. Eight millimeter, digital 8, DV, HD."

"It looks like a glorified tape player."

"It does a lot," Dave said, "but it won't capture cassette tapes."

"Who still has those, anyway?"

Dave grinned. "I still have all my tapes from when I was a kid. I'm kind of a hoarder."

"I would never have guessed," said Will, with a sweeping glance around the cluttered room. "You've got a lot of toys."

"More than I can use," said Dave. "If you see something you can take advantage of, I'd be happy to let you take it."

"Thanks, but I wouldn't know what to do with half this stuff."

Dave popped the DVD out and handed it back to Will. "I've captured the scene. I'll trim it up before Sunday."

"I can always count on you," said Will.

After his first experience with the helmet – which he had already begun thinking of as an Artifact – Rick had been hesitant to open the box again. He thought about taking it to an appraiser or a museum, but for some reason Rachel had kept it secret, and so did he.

The other boxes had held no surprises. In one were books and videotapes; in another, some of his old clothes, neatly folded. He wondered what had been going through her mind as she prepared so carefully for death. Had he known her at all? What had happened to destroy the confident, optimistic woman he'd been about to marry?

When he finally did open the box again, it was because he could no longer stand the sound of the humming. At first, he had dismissed the noise as his mind playing tricks on him. He knew this made no sense – why had he opened the box in the first place? – but he told himself it was a mental imbalance, a symptom of his deep and sudden grieving. If it were a real sound (he argued with himself), I would become habituated to it over time. It would fade into the background, gradually diminishing until I was no longer conscious of its presence.

But it did no such thing. Instead it grew louder and more insistent, with the building resentment of an itch one had determined to ignore. He thought about seeing a doctor, a psychologist, to relieve some of the building pressure.

He even considered the possibility that Rachel had simply been unable to take the sound anymore, that she had been driven mad to the point of taking her own life. He felt he was reaching a breaking point, himself.

So he finally opened the box.

The helmet, the Artifact, waited just as he had left it, surrounded by foam, protected from contact. In profile, he thought it had a vaguely sphinx-like quality, with a hint of a headdress and a barely defined ridge – it could have been a sculpted serpent – coming down the center of the forehead.

He had no way to determine its age. It was in an ancient Egyptian style, certainly. But the eyepiece – whether it was binoculars or some sort of telescope – seemed to indicate a more recent origin. Had the Egyptians invented lenses? He did not know offhand, but he doubted it.

He took the helmet out of the box, wanting to take a closer look at the eyepieces. The sound of humming faded as soon as his fingers came in contact with the cold metal, and instantly he felt a warm tingling in his hands. The effect grew stronger when he touched the eyes themselves. Like an electric charge, he thought. Was it powered somehow? This would indicate a much more recent origin than Ancient Egypt. He turned it over and looked inside. It was roughly formed to fit the face, with impressions for the nose and the mouth. The interior was the same smooth gold as the exterior, except for the two holes bored out for the eyes. Without putting the helmet on, they were mere black shadows that revealed nothing.

He examined the outside again, for the first time noticing that from this side, there were no visible holes; the eyepieces were smooth. They protruded and could be turned – without putting the helmet on, he turned both back and forth, like knobs – but they seemed to fit seamlessly into the mask, and there were no visible openings of any kind.

See-through metal? he thought, incredulous. Transparent gold? He put his face right up next to it, almost pressing his eyeball against the cylinder. Detail blurred. His eye watered. But he saw nothing but unbroken gold.

He started to put it on, then stopped, afraid. His heart was hammering, the image of Rachel in his mind, but it was far more than that. It was dangerous. He *knew* it, that the Artifact was dangerous; he could hear the terrified voice in his head, a voice he imagined to be panicked and out of breath: We've—seen—nothing—like—this—before—we—must—fear—the—unknown.

But another voice, urgent and insistent, said, *Bite the bullet. Put it on.*

—Rachel!— argued the first voice. He could see it, like a frightened angel sitting on his right shoulder.

It didn't hurt you before, argued the insidious demon that smirked on his left. *The best way to learn about it is to put it on and see what happens.*

He realized he was grinning. Smirking like the demon.

He slid the helmet onto his head.

As before, its weight seemed to disappear. Now both eyes were crystal clear, focused on the box, empty except for the Styrofoam it had been lined with.

He saw no sign of Rachel, and after several seconds passed without her appearance his heart began to quiet. He resisted the temptation to twist the left lens, wanting to look closely first before he made adjustments. The glass must have been incredibly clean. He saw no particles, smudges. No glare or light flares. And he wondered, how is it possible to see so clearly through what appeared to be polished metal on the other side?

Finally, he allowed himself to turn the knob on the right eye, testing the focus, expecting the image to lose focus. Instead, something totally unexpected happened: the right eye blurred momentarily, but then came into focus on a different scene – that is, somehow he was now looking into two entirely different rooms. His left eye still showed the empty guest room. Nothing unusual about that. Still looking into the open box. But his right eye saw black walls, flickering torchlight, and another box, much larger, carved from a dense, solid stone, smooth as marble.

He closed his left eye, shutting out the view of his house completely.

Amazing, he thought. He seemed to be in a dark, damp cave. The illusion was complete and convincing.

He closed his right eye, opened his left eye.

He was back home.

He opened both eyes. He was in two places at once. He moved his head, looking to one side, then the other. Both rooms moved, tracking his vision. It was disorienting enough to cause a feeling of nausea, and he suspected if he went very long that way he'd end up with a splitting headache.

Then he heard voices, quiet at first, and as they got louder he realized he could only hear them in his left ear. He couldn't make out words, but it sounded like they were approaching, echoing off the stone walls. He turned, parallel views rushing by, and saw an entranceway carved in the space behind him.

He could hear inside the cave, just through the left ear, and he tried to make sense of it but could not. Somehow, with his left eye and left ear, he was sensing something else, another place. The physics professor within him was baffled but made half-hearted attempts at an explanation: interior video display, cameras, a hidden earpiece feeding from a remote microphone.

But all such explanations ceased when men appeared in the door of the cave, looking past him – through him – their conversation uninterrupted. They were dressed in cloth wrapped around their waists, their chests bare, their bodies marked with either tattoos or makeup. They took no notice of Rick, as if they didn't see him. The one in the center – there were five men – carried what appeared to be the same Egyptian helmet Rick was wearing, its face toward him, the shadows that were its eyes seeming to dance with the reflection of the flickering torches.

The man with the helmet walked right through Rick, carrying the Artifact directly through his chest. To his own eyes, solid matter passed through solid matter. He felt no pain, but his nipples hardened and goosebumps rose on his arms, and at the same moment, in his left eye (which still looked at his own room) the image of Rachel appeared, kneeling over the box she had left. She blinked into existence, then dis-appeared again a moment later.

But with her arrival had come the arrival of something else… A shadow, is how he would always think of it. Rachel brought it with her, he knew, though there was no evidence to connect the two. They appeared in the same breath, and he would forever link them.

Rachel disappeared. But the shadow, something large, something behind him, grew bigger and blacker, in both eyes. Two different places, the same shadow, something so large it blocked out all light.

He wrenched the helmet from his head, gasping, short of breath, alone in the empty room.

On his way home from Dave's house, Will got a call from his sister, Cassie. She said, "You're not driving, are you?"

"No," he lied.

"You sound like you're driving."

"I can multitask," he said.

"*Can*, yes. But you aren't very good at it."

"Nobody's even on the road."

"Call me back when you get home."

He called her back while heating up a TV dinner. "Did you need something?"

"Well..." She drew the word out and dropped it slowly, forcing him to grab for it.

"I've got time," he said. "No plans."

"Okay, I don't know if I need your help so much as maybe your advice? I have this meeting in two days and I don't know what to say."

"What's the meeting about?"

"Mom didn't tell you?"

"I haven't talked to Mom."

"But you know I got hired for that movie?"

"Yeah. How many times have we talked about it?"

"I don't know. But that's what it's about."

"I thought you were supposed to be generating material?"

"Yeah, that's the problem." She dragged an exaggerated sigh from the clutches of despair. "It's not *done* yet, I mean, they're still filming. But they've given me scenes."

"Have you composed anything?"

"Anything?" she repeated. "Barely anything. Not enough."

"What about the theme a day? I thought you were preparing in advance?"

"I know you said that," she said, "but it didn't last. That seemed so random, you know? Disconnected. I get what you were saying, but I just... I mean, I just didn't feel inspired. I did maybe four days?"

"What about those?"

She sighed again. "I haven't even really looked at those."

"You wrote them down?"

"Recorded them," she said. "I didn't do so much themes as little cues." Her tone turned thoughtful. "Maybe one of those would work. I'll have to go back and listen."

Will swallowed a chunk of Salisbury steak before answering. "That was weeks ago. If you'd kept it up, you'd have like fifteen cues."

"Yeah, yeah."

"Have you turned on the keyboard?"

She huffed. "Yes. That's not the problem." Then sheepish. "But I haven't turned on the workstation. I mean the keyboard is fine but it's just improvising. I've improvised to one of the scenes like nine times."

"So record it."

"I *know*. That's what the workstation is for, duh. But I didn't turn it on, they never seemed like they were going anywhere."

"Record them anyway."

"Yes, fine!" She paused. "But what am I supposed to say in this meeting? With lessons and my classes, I have maybe three or four usable hours before then. One or two random cues isn't enough." As she was talking, the doorbell rang.

"Hold on," Will said. It had to be Rick, he thought, and it was. "Rick's here," he told Cassie. "Let me call you back."

"No hurry," said Rick, waving his hand in silent permission: *go ahead, talk to your sister*.

"Hi, Rick!" shouted Cassie, loud enough Rick could hear her.

"Hello Cassie," he said, sounding cheerful, but Will thought he looked agitated, already starting to pace even before Will put the phone back to his ear.

"I can call you back," he told Cassie again.

"I need your help!"

"I'll call you back." She was silent. "Go record a cue," Will said, "and I promise I'll help you after Rick leaves. Maybe an hour."

"Fine," she said.

"I said no hurry," said Rick after he had hung up.

"I know, I know."

"What does she need?" Rick said.

"She's struggling with a movie."

Rick's brow wrinkled. "I thought she composed music for commercials."

"Usually. This is her first movie."

"Anything worth seeing?"

"It's a local independent thing." But he could tell Rick had already lost interest. He waited until Rick sat down on the couch, then chose the seat in the chair across from him. Rick crossed his legs like it pained him, right ankle over left knee, leaning back and pointing a black Ostrich cap toe in Will's direction. "You seem agitated."

Rick shook his head. "No."

"You've been using the Artifact?"

"I don't want to talk about that right now," Rick said, impatient.

"All right."

"It's all you ever think about," Rick said.

"That's not true."

"You always bring it up. I shouldn't have told you about it."

"I thought you didn't want to talk about it."

"No, I don't. I just came to hang out."

"All right."

"I'm struggling with my book." The Ostrich cap tapped empty air a few times. "I haven't told you about it yet."

"You always struggle," Will said, "but you always finish. This one won't be any different."

"I should stay away from philosophy," Rick said, talking but not really listening. "Why even bother? It's a vast and often interesting land of opinions, but in the end everyone can make up whatever metaphysics they want. So convoluted. So much wasted time and wasted space on things that are impossible to prove, and worse, *unnecessary*! Does no one in philosophy or religion seen the value of Ockham's razor? If they did, we'd have cut God out of the equation centuries ago." He paused deliberately before asking, "Did that offend you?"

"No."

"Do you know who Ockham is?"

"Yes."

"When I work on my book, I always feel like it will offend you."

"Me?" said Will, surprised. "You don't have to worry about offending me. Come on, you're my best friend. I'm sitting here eating microwave Salisbury steak right in front of you."

"Yes, it's both disgusting and rude." He smiled when he said it, otherwise Will wouldn't have been sure he was joking.

"But we're best friends."

"Yes."

"So if you're worried about your book because of me, forget it. Let's be real, I'm only going to read it if you make me anyway."

"It's not that, I wouldn't worry about that. I don't worry about people like you, either. Religious people, I mean."

"I work at a church," said Will.

"That's what I meant."

"That doesn't mean I'm like other religious people."

"You believe in God."

"Well, yes."

Rick frowned, his eyes sharp, his jaw hinged off to one side. "My book argues against the existence of a God."

"If you feel that necessary," Will said.

"I do," said Rick. "It's irrational. How can we – as a society – make rational choices when we continue to allow ourselves to be subjugated to irrational causes?"

"Irrational causes?"

"Yes!" said Rick. "Service to an invisible higher power? What else would you call that?"

Will, caught somewhere between irritation and amusement, took his plate and fork into the kitchen to dispose of them. When he returned Rick said, apologetic, "I'm not calling you irrational."

"I didn't take it that way," said Will.

"But see, that's what I worry about when I write," said Rick. "Offending you."

"Who said I was offended?"

"I can tell," said Rick.

"Anyway," Will said, "all the times you've used the Artifact, you've never seen anything that makes you think there's a God?"

"The Artifact again?"

"Just answer the question!" Will demanded.

"No, I haven't! In fact, just the opposite: I've been searching for evidence of Jesus, and there just isn't any. I've been to all the right places at all the right times, I haven't seen a single divine man."

"That's your proof there's no God? That you can't find Jesus?"

"Aren't you a Christian?"

"Sure," said Will, exasperated.

"So you think God and Jesus are the same thing, right?" Will could tell Rick was working extra-hard to keep any hint of judgment from his tone. He failed.

"The same thing?" repeated Will. "Not the same thing."

"But both God, correct?"

"Don't try to simplify my beliefs," said Will.

"But you're a *Christian*," Rick said earnestly. "You said so yourself."

"But I don't think I'm whatever *you* think that is."

"That's one of the problems with religion," said Rick. "You can make it mean whatever you want."

"I don't think that's true."

"There's no interest in proof," said Rick, "or measures. There is much in the way of justification but little to no verification. How are we supposed to make a better tomorrow if we can't verify our basic assumptions about how things operate?"

"Is it about making a better tomorrow?"

"Isn't it?" demanded Rick. "Or at least it's about doing something together to improve the lot of the whole. Can you argue with that?" He didn't give Will a chance to. "As a scientist, I value independent thinking. But what's the usefulness of it, that's what I want to know. All this philosophical, artsy-fartsy, religious or spiritual independence... What a waste of time! Is God a woman? Was Mary a virgin? Did the Buddha achieve some kind of blissful, empty nirvana? Did the Egyptians worship cats or aliens? How could

Jonah survive in a whale? What did Jacob really wrestle with, some kind of demon? Did Jesus raise himself from the dead? You know what all these questions have in common?"

Will waited a moment – just to make sure it wasn't rhetorical – then shook his head no.

"They're pointless," said Rick. "Knowing the answers to any of these things wouldn't make one bit of difference. When are we going to evolve past this kind of thing?"

"What's really bothering you?" Will said, moving to sit next to his friend. Rick met his eyes, but Will could see a distance there, an invisible shade that Rick thought he hid behind, but Will saw the stress and the worry – he didn't know what it was about – but he said, "You haven't been like this... I haven't seen you like this in years."

"I don't know what you mean," Rick said, but he looked away, down at his feet. He uncrossed his legs and took a deep breath, leaning back into the couch. He fidgeted in various ways, not looking at Will, but Will waited quietly. Finally: "Why do humans struggle so with death?"

Rick tried to ask this flippantly, like the others, but it came out with an earnestness that brought an embarrassed sadness to his face.

"Do you struggle with it?" Will almost asked, but he

didn't; instead he thought for a moment and said, "We just want it to mean something. You care about so many things in life, you make so many decisions. We don't want it to end before we know what it means."

Rick looked him in the eye again. Still the veil was there, but Rick's face had loosened, his jaw was slack, his gaze was raw and exposed despite his attempts to maintain distance. As though he realized this, Rick brought his hand up to cover his face, to scratch at his chin as though in thought.

"It doesn't mean anything," he said sadly, after a moment. Everyone has their story, I suppose–" (here his breath hitched momentarily in the slightest of pauses) "but they're just that in the end. Stories. They might as well be fiction."

"I don't believe that," said Will.

"Does it help?" Rick said, part serious, part making fun. "I suppose you choose to believe it means something. That fills the void?"

"Can we know, one way or the other?" Will said.

"If there's a God?"

"Not even that," said Will. "If there is any meaning at all. You say there is none. You *know* this? With assurance?"

"I have no proof," Rick said.

"But it's what you believe?"

Rick shrugged and avoided the question again: "I

have no proof."

"So if you can't *know* there is no meaning, why wouldn't you take it where you can find it?"

"That's the problem," said Rick. "I can't find it."

"I can't help you there," said Will.

"What you have... this blissful faith, this unshakable conviction... you realize it's not real, right?" When Will didn't reply immediately, he unconsciously adopted a more condescending tone, leaning closer, his voice becoming that of the professor lecturing the student. "When you die, everything you've done will fade away to nothing. You will not be carried away on the wings of angels, to watch and inspire from above. You will not join a host of singing choirs that reside in celestial mansions singing Kumbayah in eternal harmony. It doesn't happen that way." He was moving gradually from professor to actor, a transition punctuated by his decision to stand, looming over Will and gesticulating with both arms. "The work you've done for others, the art you've made for yourself, your family, your music, all of it will be gone. Your sister's compositions? Those will be gone. Your church? It won't last forever." He pointed at Will like this next bit was especially important: "Your concept of God will die with you, don't you see that? Jesus – if he ever existed – died like the rest, and eventually his memory will, too."

"That's what your book's about?" Will said.

"No. Maybe." Rick grinned suddenly, his tension easing noticeably. "I don't know. I should have known you wouldn't really be offended, I just know you don't agree."

"We don't have to agree on everything."

"That's good, since as long as I've known you we've hardly ever agreed on anything." Rick started to sit back down, then said, "You have anything to drink?" and without waiting for an answer went into the kitchen. "Water's fine," he said, getting a cup out of the cabinet and filling it from the dispenser on the refrigerator. He came back into the living room, took a big drink, and said, "Are you going to call your sister back?"

"I will," said Will, "but it's not urgent. She's got time. She's just panicking because she's not using it well."

"People generally don't," Rick acknowledged. There was silence then, as they both drifted into their own thoughts about time, each dwelling on their experiences with the Artifact, each – unknown to the other – thinking what a mockery it made of time and the way people conceived of it. It made no sense, time, as endless as it was, and yet how constantly there was too little of it. It caused Rick to apologize: "I didn't mean to get into an argument, waste your time like that." Will thought, he did mean to, that's exactly why he came over. But now he's over it; now he regrets it.

"I enjoyed it," Will said. He really had; it was probably why Rick, who liked to argue, valued him as a friend.

"I should go home and write," said Rick, "instead of talking it out." He waved away Will's objection, taking his unfinished water back into the kitchen before he took his leave. But it turned out he wasn't ready to go quite yet. He stood in the entrance to the kitchen, his expression now more relaxed, but looked at Will searchingly, for the first time seeming to have a real curiosity. "What do *you* think, though?" he asked, hands in his pockets. Will still sat on the couch, looking up at him. "I mean, what's the meaning in *your* life?" A question like that, coming from Rick, often would have been a criticism. Now he was just searching.

"Everything has meaning," Will said, and he could see by the slight crunching of Rick's eyebrows that wouldn't be enough. "I watch the things that happen in my life, and I don't know what most of them mean, but I'll look back at them later and I'll realize there was something there. A message, or an answer to a question I'd been struggling with. The older I get, the more I see them, sometimes right away – I think, that's the answer I've been looking for. I guess it's easy… I guess it's common to think of all these little things as coincidences." He could see Rick thinking this. "But maybe cause and effect isn't so simple as it appears, maybe it's about something more. I think maybe cause and effect are some kind of question and answer from God, and that somewhere in there we can learn more and more of our purpose. Rick, don't you feel like you have a purpose?"

"I want to," Rick said after a moment.

"Look at your mind, your skills. I mean, I believe in physics – gravity is gravity, you can't break the laws of physics. But if everything was set... if everything was already set in stone, in some kind of predetermined plan... then what is accident? What is coincidence? The results of some law we don't know about yet, right? No, I don't know about that. Or if it is like that, maybe those aren't so much laws as angels. Do I believe in angels? I don't know. But if I do they're not the ones that have wings and carry harps. But maybe they carry purpose." He paused, thinking, this is why Rick thinks I'm an idiot. Trying to explain himself, he had lost all cohesion. But he finished anyway: "And if angels carry purpose, I think that's what people do, too. It must be part of the soul."

"You believe in life after death," Rick stated.

"I do. But I don't even know what life is, really."

Rick smiled, the easy smile of old friendship, and Will shrugged, grinning back. "Who does?" said Rick. "You have given me an idea for another book," he told Will, "thank you."

"What about the one you're working on?"

"It will work itself out," Rick said. "They always do."

After he left, Will called Cassie back. It took an effort; the conversation with Rick, though brief, had sapped his energy, and first he lay down on the couch – just to take a breather, he told himself – but when he felt himself drifting to sleep he pulled himself up limb by limb, like a marionette, until he was standing. By the time she answered he had gotten a second wind.

"Don't bother me," she said, "I'm in the middle of working," and she pretended to hang up. But then: "Thank you, by the way. I've gotten three cues done. I'm feeling much better. I think I may really enjoy this. I've never done horror before, and when you think about it, there's not a lot of demand for suspense cues in advertising. But these chords are so easy, I think eighty percent of the last one I did was diminished sevenths. Who'd have thought one sound could go so far?"

"It's a product of the ratios," Will said. "I'm glad it's going well."

"I suppose I could quit for the night," she said. "But why? When you're in the flow, you're in the zone, you shouldn't shut off the faucet. That's my opinion."

At about that same time – roughly – God was creating

the heavens and the earth, and he took a moment to agree with Cassie. It was the third day and so far all was going exceptionally well. He had started with light and discovered it to be good. Very good. Now he was bringing forth plants yielding seed, and fruit trees of every kind. He contemplated these things, and thought, when you're in the flow, when you're in the zone, you shouldn't shut off the holy faucet. So far, all was good.

Evians had no classes on Wednesday and took advantage of the opportunity to stay home. He promised himself he would avoid any type of work the entire day. Still, he couldn't resist logging onto the simulation server later in the afternoon. He had set up a test particle collision between two synchrons nested between photon pairs. The simulation showed, within a narrow collision angle, the synchrons being stripped from the protons and ejected in opposite trajectories, entangled.

Exactly as he had been hoping.

But freeing one of the synchrons was only half the battle, and besides, this was only a simulation. The practical limitations of the laboratory made isolating even a photon a challenge. Not that that would be necessary, strictly speaking, or even desirable.

Instead, Evians figured, they would want a spray of photons. A laser, in fact. Two lasers, beams intersecting at the narrow angle indicated by the simulation.

He thought on that as he put a beef pot pie in the oven. He did not consider microwaving it, though that would have shaved an efficient eleven minutes off the cooking time. Microwave ovens were on a list of items he secretly considered dangerous and half-heartedly avoided. He wasn't paranoid, but he *was* a scientist, and he was well aware of the damage microwaves could do. Probably responsible for my bad vision, he thought for the hundredth time, squinting at the oven timer.

He returned to his computer and opened his synchron collision simulation. He expanded the particle system, creating beams of intersecting lasers. He ran the necessary calculations twice, then carefully input the required values. He was just typing in the last digit as the oven dinged, and he smiled, pleased with his timing. He clicked "GENERATE" and went to retrieve his pot pie.

He carried the plate back to the computer, for no reason other than to watch the progress indicator. It was calculating somewhere in the neighborhood of fourteen million photons, and would take an estimated eleven minutes to complete.

He noticed absently there was one other active simulation in the dock, and taking a closer look he saw that it was logged into his own physics class account. He checked the user name: "gdermont." He couldn't pull any Dermonts immediately to mind. He opened the details of the simulation, which showed a status of "COMPLETED." Apparently "gdermont" had left it running and departed before it finished processing. It was a common practice with larger simulations.

Interesting, he thought, looking at the values. The particles looked remarkably similar to synchrons. An instant later he recognized the data, lifted almost entirely from his paper on the attractive force of synchrons. Finally, his mind came up with the name of the student: Gary Dermont. The one with the theory of time travel. Apparently, he was attempting to duplicate the simulation that had led Evians to write his own discourse.

Time travel, Evians chuckled. Leave it to the young. Like the Holy Grail and the Fountain of Youth, he considered it an article of faith, not science.

But it should be an interesting paper, he thought. Nothing wrong with speculation, when the math was rigorous.

Gary said, "Could you move a little? I can't see the

TV."

"Are you watching or studying?" Ben said. "If you're going to sit at the desk I'm not going to worry whether I'm in your way or not."

"Fine," said Gary, "I'm watching." He shut down the computer and joined Ben on the large couch that dominated the dorm room. They were watching a basketball game between the New York Knicks and the Las Vegas Highrollers. They weren't a fan of either team, but they watched the Highrollers for rookie Duane Anthony – known as "Duane Dimes" since his point-forward days at their high school – who was finally starting to get a lot of playing time.

"D-squared just scored," said Ben.

"I hate that nickname."

"Better than Double-D, have you heard that one?" Gary shook his head. "Sounds like a bra size," said Ben.

"It is a bra size," said Gary. "I think that's the size I found on the floor this morning."

"Probably Keri's," Ben said. "Where'd you put it?"

"Probably? You mean it could be someone else's? I kicked it under the bed. I didn't want to touch it with my bare hands."

"Got to be Keri. She was busting out of them things, too," said Ben.

"Let me watch the game please," said Gary.

"Man, we are watching the game," said Ben. Then he said, "Yeah! All right," to the TV as Dimes scored again. "Three point opportunity," he said. He nudged Gary. "Did you see that?"

"I saw that," said Gary.

"That's fingertip control."

"Yeah," said Gary, without the enthusiasm the play deserved. The mind, he was discovering, was a fickle and easily distracted mistress. When he had been sitting at the desk attempting to work he had been unable to keep his eyes off the game. Now, here in front of the TV, his mind kept drifting back to his particle simulation.

"Time out," said Ben. Captain Obvious. Ben opened the tiny dorm refrigerator and took out two cans of Coca-Cola, one for himself and one for Gary. "I'm going to go get a cup of ice," he said. "Do you want one?"

"Sure," said Gary.

Ben wandered down the hallway to where the little kitchenette had a real refrigerator with an icemaker. Idly, he wondered how close Gary was to solving his little time travel problem. Gary hadn't told him anything about it, but he'd stolen a look at one of his notebooks earlier and he had a pretty good idea that's where Gary was headed. It wouldn't surprise him if Gary did invent a time machine. He filled two glasses with ice and almost bumped into an older man coming into the kitchenette at the same time Ben was leaving.

"Excuse me," he said. "Sorry."

"No problem," said the man. He had a short goatee and moustache as white as his hair. He looked vaguely familiar to Ben, but he couldn't remember where he might have seen him before. He was too old to be a student, Ben thought at first, but it was really just the hair color that gave that impression. "Go Highrollers," said the man. "Heard you watching the game in there."

"Oh," said Ben. "Yeah, it's a good team."

"Good *player*, that Dimes kid," said the man. "Love to watch him play. One of the best ever." He smiled and winked. "They might lose this one, but that kid's a winner."

"I think they'll win this one," said Ben. "They're only down eleven."

"Maybe," the man shrugged. "I'm rooting for them."

"Me too. Later, man, don't want to miss any of the game, you know."

"Sure, later," said the man. "Catch you on the flip side."

Ben carried the cups of ice back to the room, where the game was already back in progress. "What did I miss?"

Gary looked morose. "Knicks scored twice."

"Down fifteen?" said Ben, but Gary's look said worse. "Sixteen?"

"Sixteen," confirmed Gary. "I don't think they'll win this one."

"That's what the man in the kitchen said," Ben said, and Gary gave him a questioning looking but didn't follow up on it. A second later the room's phone rang, the chirping trill indicating it was for Gary.

"Hello?" Gary disappeared into the privacy of the bathroom, dragging the cord behind him. He was in there ten minutes, while Ben watched the Highrollers lose, including several close misses by Duane Dimes in the fourth. He told Gary about it when he came out of the bathroom, but Gary brushed it off.

"I get to use the lab," he said, excited. "That was Dr. Evians on the phone. He's giving me access to all the physics facilities, I just have to schedule online." Gary was gazing into space, his mind elsewhere, basketball forgotten. "I have to get on the computer," he said. "Dr. Evians was looking at my simulation. I haven't even seen the results yet."

Ben said, "Are they going to let you make your time machine?"

Gary glared at him. "How do you know about that?" he said. "Have you been looking in my notebooks?" He pointed a finger at Ben. "You need to ask me before you look in my notes."

"Can I read your notebook?" said Ben.

"No," said Gary absent-mindedly, already thinking of

other things. "Those calculations could be very dangerous in the wrong hands."

PART TWO

The Crucible & the Cross

Will looked through space and time to a moment he had previously assumed to be fantasy. Before him was the Minotaur: a naked, muscle-bound man with ferocious eyes and massive horns protruding from his brow, his torso attached centaur-like to the thick body of a bull. He had imagined it differently somehow – head of a bull attached to a man – but instead at this imagining the Artifact took him to this creature, both majestic and disturbing. His power was evident in every slight movement, his insanity apparent in the curl of his lip and the set of his stare.

"One cannot – always – hear the remorse in the voice of the guilty," intoned a deep voice, and Will then noticed the man in the shadows. He stood behind the beast, his hand resting on the Minotaur's flank. "But one can smell the scent in the sweat of the accused. There, it cannot be hidden." The Minotaur snarled, and the voice of the man admonished him, "*Not* from hunger alone, my son. Only the bodies of the defiled."

The Minotaur grunted and spoke a word Will heard very clearly – amplified by the Artifact – but did not understand: "Allementu."

"Justice does not have favorites," the man replied. "From the givers is taken, from the taken is more taken, then all is given in the end."

"I will take *more*," said the Minotaur. His eyes raked the darkness restlessly, his nostrils flaring in a snarl that never left his face.

"You will," said the man. "But only from the defiled."

"They are *all* defiled." The monster's voice was a bellowing blend of beast and man, the words torn violently from a throat clenched tight with anger. "None have been clean." His rear hooves clicked the dull stone in staccato agitation. The sound echoed in the labyrinth.

There was another sound then, a shuffling, followed by the gentle sobs of a child. "You have been found," the man whispered, stepping back, away from the Minotaur. "The first approaches."

He disappeared into the dark at the same moment the child appeared around the corner; no, two children, twin girls, around the ages of ten or twelve, Will guessed. Both had pale olive skin and black curls cascading down to skinny shoulders. The first one saw the Minotaur and stifled a scream.

They ran, disappearing back around the corner, but the bull man lowered his head and ran after them. Will followed with a thought, a whisper of intention to the Artifact, and as he rounded the corner he saw the Minotaur grab one of the girls by the shoulder roughly, at the same time knocking the other to the ground with his free hand.

Will touched the left eyepiece of the Artifact, readying himself to enter the scene. But he resisted the immediate impulse to come to the girls' defense. What could he do? He could provide no protection for either child.

"Please," sobbed the twin who had been knocked to the ground. "Please don't hurt her."

"She is *mine* to take," the Minotaur growled.

"Please!" the girl cried. "She's my sister!"

The beast man showed no sign of sympathy, but held the other girl up, lifting her painfully by her shoulder, and glared into her face. "What do you have to say for yourself?" She flinched as spittle flew from his lips. But she sobbed too uncontrollably to reply, and after a moment he threw her down with the other. They huddled together, staring up at him, too afraid to attempt another escape. "Your *name*?" the Minotaur yelled at the first child.

"Melina," she said.

"Your name?" he repeated, to the second girl.

"Zona," the first girl spoke again. "Her name is Zona." The girl moved to protect her sister. "She can't speak."

The Minotaur snorted, shaking his horns. "Because she is full of lies," he said. He made a threatening move toward her, and Will could no longer keep from turning the eyepiece. He felt the sickening rush of displacement. He heard the echo of the clapping sound that accompanied his appearance, and the Minotaur turned, startled.

"Let them go," Will said. He kept his fingers to the eyepiece, ready to escape at any moment. But the bull did not attack. Instead, he raised his face high and sniffed the air, a growl rising in his throat. Before he could speak, the man in the shadows appeared behind him. In his haste to protect the girls, Will had not taken him into account.

"From where have you come, traveler?" The man kept his distance from Will, aligning himself with the Minotaur, laying a gentle hand on its back.

"Who are you?" Will asked. The man stepped into the light, and Will saw beneath his hooded cloak a black beard, curled hair going to grey, thick brows curled above eyes of piercing blue. The man held a staff in front of him like a badge of privilege.

"From where, and from whence, traveler?" the man demanded, his voice tinged with impatience. "I smell the burning of years between us. Its oil is not like any other."

"I'm from the future," Will said. He assumed this was true. "A place you could not possibly have heard of."

"Voice from the future," mused the old man, sniffing the air as though it would reveal the truth. "Name this place." Behind him the Minotaur growled, baring his teeth at Will, and the two girls crept away, back into the dark of the maze.

"San Joseph," said Will.

"He is defiled!" the Minotaur hissed.

"Quiet, boy," the man chided him, and the Minotaur bowed his head. The man leaned his staff toward Will. "Is this land, San Joseph, a just land?"

"Tell me your name," said Will, "and I will tell you about it."

"Minos," he said. And, good to his word, Will told him things of San Joseph. Not of the technology, the scientific wonders, but instead of what the people were like, about his work. A typical day in San Joseph. They

87

talked so long that the bull man finally wandered away in boredom. Minos was a judge, he told Will, and he had been blessed by the gods. What did that mean? Will wanted to know. They showed favor to his plans, Minos said, provided they were just. They worked miracles upon his need. Minos was surprised to discover there were no gods in San Joseph, or, as Will would have it, that there was one God, but he did not appear to bless the righteous or punish the accused. Minos, who had spoken to Zeus – a mighty giant of a man who came down to earth upon thunderclouds – did not know what to make of this god. Will did not know what to think of a man who flew down from the sky. Did he have a ship? he asked. A chariot? But Minos said he rode a horse made of lightning whose hooves struck the clouds like thunder.

What would the Minotaur have done with the children? This Will was afraid to ask, but eventually did. Eaten them, said Minos. It was the purpose for which he was created. Minos did not seem disturbed when he told Will this. He said it with the simplicity of fact, the irrefutable certainty of law. But Will was much disturbed when finally he turned the knob and returned to Rick's cottage.

Rick did not ask him what he had seen or whom he had spoken to; it was like a rule understood between them. But he frowned when he took the Artifact and put it back into the case, as though he regretted allowing Will to touch it.

The first time Rick had let Will use the Artifact he told him, "You control it with your mind." But to Will that had never seemed true. It did seem like if he thought about a place, or time, or even a concept, then then helmet would respond by taking him there when he turned the lens. But in *another* way, what seemed like really happened was he turned the lens and looked into the glass and saw millions of scenes, and then, like a Ouija board, his subconscious took control of his fingers and decided what he stopped on.

In other words, Will couldn't really control it; in a way it seemed like it controlled him.

But perhaps for Rick it was different. Will's own mind was chaotic, creative, unorganized. But the lightning speed of Rick's thinking seemed a different breed; he imagined Rick's mind as a room full of filing cabinets, not a scrap of paper out of place. Maybe for Rick it was a cleaner, simpler process, a matter of picturing Victorian England and the next moment chatting with the Queen over tea.

For Will, there were unexpected sensations, visual artifacts, and a frequent heady, altered sense of displacement. Rick had never spoken in detail of the experience, instead – like the professor he was – he doled out snippets of instruction and information without personal commentary. Will recognized that it was simply too big to talk about. Like many another powerful experience, it could only be shared directly.

Physically, the helmet was simple to operate. By turning the right eyepiece Will was able to seek out any scene he could imagine, allowing him to look through space and time. The left eyepiece, on the other hand, seemed joined to the first; when he turned it to focus, he actually *moved* through space and time – or something – and transported into the scene he had viewed through the right lens. By turning the left lens out of focus, he went back, returning to his original location, and even – it seemed to Will – returning to the original time. He had watched Rick using it many times, and each time Rick had turned the left eyepiece, he had turned it back immediately. Will assumed, then, no matter how long he was gone in the Artifact, no time passed back in the cabin.

It raised all manner of questions about existence, space, and time that Will was unprepared to answer. But his experiences had been getting stranger and stranger; the visit to the Labyrinth and the conversation with Minos made him think he knew nothing about the nature of reality.

But these were questions for Rick to deal with, he

thought. Rick was the scientist, the physicist, the experimenter. Will considered himself a simpler man and did not let such questions disturb him; he decided only that the experience was unique – the Artifact was unique – and he was determined to enjoy it.

But as he drove to church on Sunday morning he couldn't stop thinking about the girls, the twins the Minotaur had no doubt devoured. How many? he wondered. How many children had fed his insatiable hunger? How many bones lay buried within a Labyrinth that was yet to be found?

And didn't he, having seen it, and even having the ability to return, bear some responsibility in this terrible ritual?

He thought over this as he conversed with Marianne, who always arrived early to bring donuts and prepare the coffee. He was only half-listening, and realized after a moment she was waiting for him to answer a question he hadn't heard.

"Say that again," he said.

"Do you know anyone who might be able to cover the nursery?" she said, unperturbed. Then, when he still looked lost, "on Wednesday night? I have to pick my niece Clarissa up from the airport."

"What about Karen or Mackenzie?"

"I asked them already, they're not available."

"Okay," said Will, "I'll figure it out." In his mind he was picturing the Minotaur, re-examining its size, thinking he must be remembering it wrong, exaggerating it. But the memory was still vivid. He could still see the tiny girl clutched in the monster's giant hand. Still see as both girls were thrown around like tiny dolls.

"It's really exciting," said Marianne, "I haven't seen her in months, since the summer. She helped out at the theater. She's really good with lights and sound but she doesn't really take it seriously. What do you think that would be like for a job? Is there money in that, do you think? Of course that's what she's worried about. But I don't really think she has it in her to be a psychologist. I know I shouldn't say so, but. She's no counselor."

"But if it's what she wants to do," said Will.

"I don't know if that's it so much as she thinks it'll make money. Everybody needs therapy, she says."

"There's some truth to that," Will remarked. He was thinking, the next time he put on the Artifact he would go back to the same place and see what he could do about the kids getting eaten. It was a sacrifice, Minos had said, an atonement for wrongdoing. *Just*, he called it. *Justice*. Not in this day and age, thought Will. Nowadays nothing was as beloved as children. What about justice for the defenseless? he thought.

"Yes, but she's not a very good listener," Marianne said. "You can't be a very effective therapist if you don't listen. I've tried to tell her that."

"But she doesn't listen," Will said, smiling through distracted thoughts. Marianne chuckled. Would it be possible to take a weapon? is what Will was wondering. A sword may be nothing to a Minotaur, but what about something like an automatic rifle? Of course this was idle fantasy; Will had never owned a gun had no clue how he would go about acquiring such a thing.

"Maybe you can talk to her next Sunday. I'll bring her with me," Marianne said. "I think you've met Claire before."

"I think I have," said Will, suddenly wanting out of the conversation, not sure why.

"Not to talk her out of being a therapist."

"Of course not," said Will.

"I don't mean that. I just mean, about theater."

"There's not a lot of money in it."

"Maybe film?" Marianne followed him back to the rehearsal room.

"Maybe," he said. "Harder to get into."

"She's just so good at it," said Marianne.

"Which means she probably enjoys it," Will said. "I'll ask her about it."

"Thank you," said Marianne.

Will didn't think there was any way Rick would let him try to take a weapon through the Artifact. Even if he could. And there was no reason to think it was even possible. He had never tried. Maybe Rick had, but if so, he hadn't told him.

"From the takers is taken," Pastor Drew said, and was pleased to see – finally – Will stir, in the second row, his head coming up as he at last appeared to be listening. "Our Savior's own mission was revealed in the Beatitudes. Eight blessings, eight promises to the poor, the meek, the hungry. But are they blessings for everyone? For what of the wealthy, the rude, or the gluttonous? You see the Lord is just, and justice does not have favorites."

Drew saw Will frowning and thought, good, good. He's listening. He looked to the right and caught the eye of Paul, then Stan, then Nan and Stacy and Rodney. The two kids were both playing on the same cell phone; everyone else was raptly attentive.

"He is not a cruel God. There is no cruelty in the Lord. But He sent his Son to bring justice to those who received none from *people*. He sent our Savior to bring justice to *us*. If!

"If we are poor in spirit. If we mourn." He paused dramatically after each sentence, wanting them to think about each word, letting his gaze move through four faces between each sentence – Tim, Janet, Trish, Malcolm – willing them to consider the importance of what he was saying. "If we remain meek." – Barbara, Erin, Pete, Candace – "If we are merciful." – Tom, Jevon, Bobby, Amber – "If we are peacemakers." – Harry, Nathan, Jeffrey, Karen – "If we hunger for *righteousness*. If we are persecuted for *righteousness*."

He stepped back, up two steps, nearer to the podium – though he would not stand behind it – and placed his hand gently upon the Bible that rested there. "True knowledge of God," he said, "true knowledge of the *justice* of God, is an understanding of righteousness. We give our devotion to the Lord, this is what He asks of us. But the Lord Himself is devoted to justice."

He paused, momentarily forgetting his next bullet point, using the dramatic space to search, search... Then, "If you give, unto you will be given. If you believe in Him, He will have equal faith in you. If you are greedy, then others will covet, they will steal from you. If you are unkind, then others will wish to be cruel to you. What others have called karma is in fact the Lord's justice, the Lord's protection of the vulnerable. It exists in the reality of heaven and the reality of hell. But it exists equally in the here and the now, if only we can understand, if only we can strive to emulate the way of the Savior in our own manner of living. To the peacekeeper will be given peace."

He saw several heads nodding and felt pleased, but knew the message was unlikely to be wholly received. But every bit mattered. "For every choice, there is a just reward. Without justice," he said, beginning his wrap-up, "all worship is useless. Without actions that are wholly righteous in the eyes of the Lord, all other sacrifices are wasted. All other riches are bankrupt."

Duane Dimes, rookie star of the Las Vegas Highrollers, was not at church that Sunday morning. They had flown before sunrise after a late game in Houston. Instead, he woke up early to watch Morning Lighthouse, but then found himself struggling to pay attention. He could not get his mind off his performance in the previous night's game.

"It was awful," he said aloud, as an apology to the universe. "*I* was awful."

Of course he hadn't meant to be. He had put in the effort; Coach had praised him on his hustle – it was why he had played over thirty minutes for the first time this season – but he had made only one of thirteen shots and that wasn't going to cut it on any night against any team, let alone in an away game in the first round of the playoffs.

"Let's bow our heads and listen to the Word of the

Lord in song," Jared Flack said on the TV, and Duane tried to clear his mind and do that as the Tabernacle Choir sang: "Let all who take refuge rejoice in you, let them ever sing for joy." They repeated the refrain, and he found himself singing along – or at least humming the tune. But he was picturing the rim, reviewing a mid-ranger where Reggie Neal – they called him the Creature because his arms were so long – had gotten a hand into his eyes, so he had lifted a little higher; he had seen it clearly enough. Felt fine on the release. Reggie didn't even touch his elbow. So what was it? Well, nothing had seemed fluid the whole night. He had never really connected, never really felt in the flow.

The phone rang and he almost didn't answer, but he looked at it, saw it was his Mama, and how could he not? He didn't want to talk to her, though. He knew what she was going to say.

"You did good," but her tone said he was twelve and it was just a scraped knee. "You did really good."

"I was terrible, Mama, get out of here with that."

"You always feel that way when you lose, honey."

"And what's a moms going to say that's anything different than, 'You did good, son, you did really good.' I shot one for thirteen, how good is that?"

"You *did* do good. Six rebounds? Three assists? Leroy got four boards, did you see that? Four? And he's seven one."

"That was matchups, that wasn't his fault. He had Perkins drawing him out." He paused. "We've got to figure that out."

"Well if it's matchups for him, that's all it was for you, too. That monster in your face the whole time."

"He's the Creature, Mama, not the monster, I told you before."

"He looks like Frankenstein."

"Mama, that's not nice. That's not why they call him the Creature, I told you."

"You played a lot," she said. "You got over thirty minutes."

"We lost."

"Well that's not what they're talking about here." Referring to his home town in Ohio. "Here they're talking about the Highrollers might have a chance. Here they're talking about you."

"Talking about one for thirteen.

"You always say it's not about the numbers," she said. "Anyways, you watching Morning Lighthouse?"

"Of course."

"I knew you'd be up for that. That Flack, he cuts a figure."

"C'mon, Ma."

"If he wasn't a religious man, I got a feeling he could be quite the dancer. You've heard him sing, right?"

"He's a man of God, Mama," Duane said

reproachfully. "I'm going to let you go so I can listen to the sermon."

"Yes, you pay attention," she said. "I'm proud of you."

Proud of me for what? he thought. I'm a ball player. Who just lost.

"The lost will be found," said Jared Flack, just as Duane looked at the TV. A close up of his eyes, intent, solemn, seeming to look right into Duane's soul. "The repentant will be saved."

Highrollers lost last night," Ben told Gary, as if he didn't know. "Dropped the first one." They were rooting heavily for the unexpected sixth seed to push their way to a highly unlikely championship, and losing the first game of the playoffs did not help their chances.

"How did Dimes do?" Gary asked, just to make conversation. He had already checked out the box score online and it hadn't looked good. The numbers said it had been a struggle for the entire team.

Ben shrugged. "Didn't look great."

"Everybody has an off night."

"I tried to get you to watch it," Ben said. "You were out, man. I mean, out."

Gary sighed. "Heavy reading."

Ben pursed his lips, scrunched his eyebrows, shook his head. "You need to quit staying up all night. Learn to relax."

"It's this project," Gary said. "This simulation for Evians."

"Yeah, the top secret thing."

Gary gave him a suspicious look. "Who said it's top secret?"

"So what is it?"

It was Gary's turn to purse his lips and scrunch his brow. "Okay, it's top secret." What it really came down to was he didn't know how to talk about it without sounding either too technical – which Ben pretended to follow – or too vague or, worse, dreamy and ambitious.

"Well, you've been obsessing." Ben's voice was matter-of-fact. "This is a problem that needs to be fixed."

"It's a complex problem," Gary said. "Complex things require complex thought. You might call it study."

"Hard work requires a break," Ben said firmly. "It's a weekend. Last night was Saturday night, for crying out loud. There were at least three frat parties on campus. What were you doing the whole night? You were passed out on the floor by nine. Which would be a whole other thing if you had been drinking. Were you drinking? I think you had Kool Aid."

"I didn't have Kool Aid."

"Were you drinking?"

"It was Hawaiian Punch."

"Give me a break. Gary, you're the smartest person I know. You're the one who should be spending the least time studying."

Shortly after Ben left, Gary started worrying: was he taking this project too seriously?

Was he taking himself too seriously?

From somewhere in the recesses of his mind the image of Dr. Evians appeared, a memory from the moment Gary had told him about his idea. "Time travel," he had laughed. Well, it was more chuckling than laughing, but in Gary's mind now, it was a condescending chuckle, somewhat akin to shaking car keys at a baby. He had been amused, diverted, charmed with Gary's enthusiasm the way one would enjoy a toddler's naïve excitement over a simple amusement. Evians had been kind about it. But of course the idea of time travel was ridiculous.

It truly was a child's dream – Gary's childhood dream. He would never tell anyone the origin, but wasn't it what he had been working on his whole life? The childish dream of an eight year old, imagination exploding as he had read the comic Calvin and Hobbes, where Calvin had built a machine – the transmogrifier – out of a box. Calvin's transmogrifier turned things into other things. Gary had immediately built his own box machine, but instead of writing

"Transmogrifier" on his he wrote "Time Traveler." He had made his much fancier than Calvin's. Inspired by his father's collection of science fiction B-movies, he had covered the entire thing in aluminum foil, decorated it with blinking lights and stickers, even simple working circuits later when he had demanded a beginner's electronics set. He had kept it in his room all the way through high school, pretending it meant little to him but stopping any attempt to remove it.

If he were honest with himself now, all he was *really* trying to do was take a toy he had made as a child and create a real one as an adult.

That was why it was "top secret," why he wouldn't even tell Ben about it... because it was a foolish idea, doomed to fail. His experiment with Evians was well short of a "time machine." But it was all part of the same silly – and impossible – dream.

It was with no surprise, thinking these thoughts, that he opened his simulation and found that it had failed. One part of him asked the never-ending question: What next? What did we learn? What do we try next? This voice drove him to remain there, looking over results, calculating values.

But it was another voice that spoke with more conviction: Of course it failed. You are a kid playing games and calling it science. You're a dreamer and a romantic trying to camouflage your true colors with measurements and mathematics.

Good luck, kid. (Gary imagined this as the voice of God, but really it was the voice of John Wayne attached to a face that looked sus-piciously like Einstein.) Good luck, kid, the voice drawled, but remember: God don't play dice.

Rick didn't believe in God, but he too believed the universe didn't play dice. Every effect could be traced to an underlying cause (or set of causes). There was nothing in manifestation that could not be traced to a simple chain of prior physical causation, and any speculation otherwise was the irrational chasing of shadows. The mind could compare similarities in situations and look for similarities in root circumstances, but to search for meaning in the coincidental relationships beyond that was fruitless.

It was a meaningless coincidence that this young woman who now haunted his campus would share the same name as the one who had haunted his thoughts so long, he told himself, as he once again came upon the former on the bench by the tennis courts. At most it was a consequence of history and tradition, the memes of ancient culture diffused over time into commonalities. Rachel was, after all, an old and biblical name.

He thought about turning around, avoiding her. But when she saw him right away and pretended with studied deliberation that she hadn't he put on a smile and approached her: "Good morning, Rachel. How is the book?" She continued to ignore him for a second or two longer and he was angry with himself, thinking, why did I give her the opportunity?

Then she said, "Good morning, Dr. Mayliss," in a very polite tone. "It's riveting." And she turned her eyes back to the book as though to end the conversation.

Despite her dismissive tone – or more likely because of it – Rick sat down next to her on the bench. She frowned. He said, "I know I was abrupt, last time we met."

"Rude, you mean?" she said.

"Perhaps," he replied.

"Rude is when you know you're being a jerk. Did you know?"

"Yes," he said.

"Well if I was being rude, I wasn't aware of it," she said, "which means it wasn't rude." She paused, then clarified, "I was *insensitive*, yes, but not rude."

"I was both," he said.

"Yes," she said, closing her book. "You were."

"I hope you will forgive it," he said.

She turned to him on the bench, dropping her coldness, peering into his face curiously. "This other

104

Rachel, she must have really done a number on you." It bothered him, and she saw it right away – attentive to him in a way that made him self-conscious. "I'm sorry," she said. He could see she – like himself – had difficulty apologizing. "Do you not like to talk about her?"

"It's fine," he said, though it wasn't. Any other answer would be ridiculous after all this time, he thought. Sixteen years was too long to dwell on things. Too long to be sensitive about things.

"Did she leave you?" Rachel asked, inexorable. "Why did you split?"

"We didn't split," he said, then words that he hadn't spoken in a long time: "She died." Then, before she could ask another question, "She killed herself."

"Oh," she said, and her face became still as she hid her thoughts. It had been a while, but it was always the same when people found out. The sudden tension, the awkwardness as they began looking for a way out of the conversation. Was she wondering how she had done it? Was she wondering why? Was she thinking it was him, that there was something wrong with him that would make someone want to take their own life? That must be what she thought, for then she said, "Do you feel guilty?"

"Of course not," he said, too quickly. "It was her own choice. It wasn't because of me."

"But you feel guilty anyway," she said.

"No."

"Of course you do," she said, "but you're right, you shouldn't. It's no one's fault – it's a mental illness."

So they had told Rick in the support seminars Rcahel's Dad had made him attend, and he wondered if she too had known someone, if she too had attended such seminars. She said it with assurance, a canned response in the same way as the seminars. But she didn't know the other Rachel, she couldn't be sure. And he had never believed it, never believed that suicide was a kind of disease. He didn't see how you could equate a person's actions, the decisions they made, with the malfunctioning of a physical organism. The first, being chosen, was not subject to the vicarious influences of nature, while the latter – a living organism – was at the mercy of the elements from which it was created. What he said was: "I don't believe in mental illness." Rachel looked taken aback, and he said, "By calling the things people think mental illnesses it excuses the choices they make. It's a bad habit to get into, excusing bad choices."

"So you blame *her*, then."

"It was her decision," he said. He tried not to sound cold and heartless, but he got the impression it came out that way. But how could he share the depth of it, the millions of ways he had gone around the question?

Sixteen years.

She watched his eyes closely, searching for the thoughts he tried to keep hidden from his face. "Did you love her?"

"Of course," he said.

"Were you in love with her?" She asked this like it was a different question, and he became frustrated. He was already frustrated. He showed it on his face, let his hands move in an agitated manner.

"It is a clichéd phrase," he said. "It means nothing. At best, it refers to a state of mind – hormonally influenced, no doubt – that is temporary and probably equivalent to any other mental *illness*, as you called it."

"Ha!" she said. Not like he had something funny, but like an exclamation point to his thought.

"It doesn't make any sense," he said, "that an organism whose genetic inclinations are all toward survival would end its own life by choice."

"No, it doesn't," she said. Then, after a hesitation, "That's why they call it an illness."

"A failure of rationality," he said, though it had never made sense, for Rachel had been a very rational person.

"A disease," she said, "of the rational mind." She hadn't looked away from his face, and he realized, suddenly, uncomfortably, that he hadn't looked away from hers either. He glanced around at the still empty park, and she pressed on, demanding his attention. "And who says our genetic inclinations are all towards survival?" she asked. She argued with purpose, with enjoyment and the appreciation of an intellectual – so like another Rachel long ago. "What of a mother's nurturing instinct? Or of sexual attraction?" After she said the last she made a small thoughtful motion with her mouth that drew his eyes from hers, holding them as she shaped the next words: "What of those?"

"Survival of the species," he said. "It's the same thing."

"I think there are many people who would not agree with you," she said.

"Are you one of them?"

She smiled; he was still staring at her mouth, he realized, and looked up. She watched his eyes but made no acknowledgement of his reaction. "I do not disagree," she said. "Nor do I agree. I do not come to conclusions if I can avoid it."

"We're meant to come to conclusions," he said. "It's impossible to avoid it."

She turned to him on the bench, moving slightly closer, slipping her book into her purse, all in the same motion. "I think sexual attraction is nature's way of teaching us compassion," she said. "What do you think?"

"I think sexual attraction is nature's way of preserving the species," he said, his tone becoming dry and analytical, as he sought to cover his discomfort. "There is no other reason for it to have developed in an organism."

"When you put it that way, it sounds like a service to the community," she said. "How very philanthropic, this desire to rut."

"It is the result of selective breeding. An increased probability of progeny. Without sexual attraction, what would be the chances of oppositely gendered individuals of the same species engaging in the activity necessary to procreate?"

"What would be the chances, indeed?" she said, frowning. She turned to him on the bench and put a hand gently on his arm, above the elbow. It was an intimate gesture, and she looked at him to gauge his reaction. He tried to have none.

"You asked what I thought," he reminded her.

"But if you think that," she said, "then why were you in love with this Rachel so long ago?" He didn't answer. "How long ago?"

"How is sexual attraction related to compassion?" he said. "I don't get that."

"It's a transcendental experience, to love someone," she said.

"We're talking attraction, not love."

"Let me finish."

"All right."

"Why would such a powerful emotion exist, if sexual attraction was merely for rutting?" She said, "Think about it. A lot of people enjoy rutting. Most everybody, I imagine, if there weren't so many strings attached, you know?" Her hand hadn't moved from his arm. It felt relaxed and at ease. Could she feel his tension? "But love is something else again. What's the need for that? A lot of species don't form partnerships. So why would this thing exist? But think of this emotion – it would make you die for someone. This is beyond any survival instinct... This 'in love' that makes people do such crazy things."

"Mental illness," he mumbled.

"But you were in love with her," she said. "You still are."

"I don't think so." Then, "I was. It was a long time ago."

"How long?"

"Sixteen years."

"Long time," she said. Her hand squeezed his arm gently, then fled back to her lap. "And you still can't get her out of your mind."

"It's the name. It's just the name," he said. "That you, and her..."

"It's just a name," she said, and he looked up from

her hand to her eyes. Their eyes locked. She said, "It's a common name. It's Biblical, you know. You haven't known another Rachel, in all this time? All of sixteen years?"

He shook his head. "I don't think so," he said. "Not that I can remember."

"How very odd," she said. "I'm sure it's just a coincidence."

"That's all anything ever is," he said.

Henry woke up late on Sunday. The previous night he had pushed to the fine edge of daylight in his pursuit of knowledge, staying up until well after five reading translations of old Egyptian engravings. This was well outside of his usual field of study, but Henry was prone to let curiosity guide his research. In this case, it was idle at best; it had in fact arisen from his light reading, a biography on the entomologist William Sharp McLeay. It was his work in systems that had initially drawn Henry's attention. Then his interest had moved from McLeay to a particular species of dung beetle – the *scarabaeus sacer* – which MeLeay had found fascinating. It had special significance in Egyptian mythology, Henry had discovered, where it represented Khepri, the morning form of the sun god Ra, who rolled the sun across the sky. Exactly, as it turned out, the way the dung beetle known as the scarab rolled a ball of dung across the ground.

Funny, thought Henry, to compare a ball of dung to the sun. What Henry was amused by: didn't the Egyptians worship the sun? But it was all right to represent it as a ball of dung. Henry had smirked at that. But then he had looked at pictures of the scarab in engravings and had been struck by the beautiful symmetry of it. One could see their worship in their art; the majesty of the tiny creature as it held the sun aloft.

He wanted to show the pictures to someone, but it had been four in the morning and he had not wanted to wake his daughter. Instead, he had saved his favorites to the hard drive, then read for another hour, fascinated by all the crazy interpretations of ancient Egyptian symbolism that abounded on the internet.

Good night!

When he got up it was past noon, and Kristen – his daughter – was nowhere to be found. She had left a note by the computer: "not into beatles anymore, daddy, that was ages ago." He laughed at her spelling – she knew he was a big fan of the band – and only then remembered her interest in beetles. Long since faded, as she had indicated. What had inspired it? He couldn't remember. He would have to ask her if she was familiar with the scarab.

Where was she? He had to think about what day it was – Sunday – which meant she was probably at church with her friend Jenny. She used to ask him to go, but his weekends were precious to him. Did she still go? He assumed so.

He would have to ask her, he thought. When would she be home?

He didn't know. He looked around for a schedule around the kitchen, all the while thinking, where does she put stuff? I know she keeps a list. Where is her list? He was a little afraid to touch anything. He knew she kept it exactly the way she liked it. He would have to ask her where she kept her list, he thought. And her schedule. Did she keep a schedule?

He scratched at his head and wandered by her room, where the door was open. Invisible cobwebs of resistance tugged at him as he entered, so rarely did he do so. Her desk was neatly organized, her purple blankets pulled tightly around the bed. Everything in the room was purple or black. Kristen liked purple, dark purple, and had decorated the room in abstract patterns. None of the usual girl softness or boy posters for his Kristen; instead the room was a carefully constructed work of art, a bold statement of identity.

He didn't see any sign of a list or a schedule. He idly opened the top drawer of her dresser – a heavy wooden thing painted black – and immediately regretted it. It was filled with panties, many of them lacy and very feminine. He closed it quickly, but before he did he couldn't help noticing a long strip of packages that disturbed him. Rubbers. Condoms.

He felt a moment of disoriented confusion – am I in the wrong room? – and then he felt a little sick, his hand still resting on the handle of the drawer.

Was Kristen having sex?

With who? Did she have a boyfriend?

He had never met a boyfriend.

Was it worse if she didn't have a boyfriend? What if she was sleeping around? Didn't she know that was dangerous?

All of a sudden, he realized they had never had the talk. How could I not have had the talk? he thought. What kind of father doesn't have the talk?

It's usually the mother's job, he said to himself. How was I to know? How could a single father be expected to remember all such things?

But that was prevarication – excuses against the real truth: that he was a lousy father. The truth was that Kristen took far better care of him than he did her, and everyone knew it. It was a bit of a joke between the two of them. Always before, he had been amused.

Now, he felt ashamed.

What right do I have to judge? he asked himself. What right to I have to tell her what to do?

He left her room just as he had found it. He doubted he would ever enter again. When she came home that evening in her usual cheerful mood, he said nothing. He tried not to think about it. He paid more attention to her than usual, he listened with interest as she talked about church, about lunch with her friends.

He tried to look for little ways to be a better father, hoping she never noticed anything had changed. Later, she disappeared to her room. She left her door open, and he could hear her music. She was a Taylor Swift fan. "I'm going to the lab," he yelled. She didn't answer right away. He stood there, uncertain, not wanting to go near her room, but finally she poked her head out and said, "What?"

"I'm going to the lab," he said.

"All right."

"Don't wait up," he said.

"Of course not."

"Be good."

"Of course," she said smiling.

He had called the lab earlier and had James, his lab manager, get it set up for his particle experiments. He had planned on running them tomorrow, but now he needed something to clear his mind. Before he left, he called his student Gary Dermont, whose ideas had prompted the experiments. He enjoyed the boy's enthusiasm, and was pleased when he agreed to meet him in the lab that evening.

"Bring something to read," he warned. "It will take me over an hour to refine the laser, and the computations will be monstrous during the prep phases."

Instead, Gary showed up with a small portable VCR-TV combo that he explained was his roommate Ben's. "It's playoffs," he said. "I know they lost, but still, I recorded the game."

"Playoffs?" repeated Evians.

"Basketball," said Gary. "You watch?"

Evians shrugged and shook his head. "Not really into sports," he said. "I'll get started on prepping the box in a moment, but I'm going to need you to read these numbers off first, while I aim the laser." He handed Gary a small notebook with a list of values.

"Sure, no problem." He read off the numbers, watching curiously as Evians plugged them into two sets of axis controllers.

"Okay," said Evians, "now you can give me a few minutes." Gary watched at first, as the professor powered up the lasers and began making comparisons between two computer displays. The balancing turned out to be a boring process, the adjustments so minute that they did not register to the eye, each followed by a series of slow and careful alignment tests. Eventually Gary flipped on the little TV where he had set it on the side table. The game picked up just after half-time, paused the moment he had left off when Evians called.

It had gotten exciting, tied up early in the fourth, when Evians finally said, "It's ready. I've got the two lasers set to an extremely low intensity – a few photons a second – and pointed to the same spot on this barium borate crystal."

"A nonlinear optical crystal," said Gary.

"Good," said Evians, smiling.

"I was going to recommend it in my paper."

"Yes," said the professor. "It will convert the single photon from our ultraviolet laser into two oppositely polarized photons. Of course, theoretically, these two photons are governed by the same synchron, if, as simulations indicate, synchrons do not duplicate."

"Right," said Gary.

"This violet laser, on the other hand, will emit a single photon that will enter our polarizer before impacting the barium borate at the same time as the ultraviolet photon. This is governed, we presume, by a separate synchron."

"And I see you have a half-silvered mirror at the end of the photon path," Gary said. "This is exactly the way my simulation was set up."

"Yes," said Evians. "I saw no need for alterations. As you indicated, if only one of the synchrons turns out to be a homogenort, then the frequency of our violet light will be altered by the half-silvered mirror, and appear to our detector as green."

"Or," said Gary, "if two archons entangle before splitting on the mirror, the quantum wave function will uncollapse along the time dimension, creating a synchronic wormhole."

"Too speculative," said Evians. "Only the homogenort is predictable. We must first prove the existence of the synchrons, then we can start measuring their interaction." He smiled, his eyes glinting behind his glasses. "So let's prove it, shall we?" He fired up the machine. "We'll let it run for ten minutes and look at the results."

And a few short seconds later, the first ultraviolet photon split on the violet photon and turned it green.

At the same time (as measured by the synchron), a man five-thousand years earlier on the other side of the world was struck blind with visions. It became known he was mad, and when he started building machines in the dark, word spread around his Egyptian village that he was a devil who could see without light. He was a hermit, feared, who spoke in strange poetry that most took as nonsense, though some believed was prophecy.

A very brave few came to the solitary space of this

mystic madman, to ask him such questions as, "How does the ba find the ka after death?" and "Which sacrifice will the gods most favor?" and "Does Ra see our actions in the day as well as the night?"

The prophet's eyes were clear, not milky, but they never came to focus. "The gods live beneath the surface of the pool," was one answer he gave. "They see us with our own eyes when we gaze into it."

One boy on the edge of manhood wished to learn magic – to control the gods and demons, and bend them to his will – and followed the madman around, asking more personal questions. "Who were you before you had visions?"

"A boy like you."

"Did Ra give you these visions? Does your knowledge come from him?"

"It was light from the sun," the madman replied.

"Not from Ra?"

"It is the light that Ra left behind after he died." The boy mistook these words, and thought that magic was born from what he had once considered blasphemy. He walked away thinking, gods can die. And he set out to prove this by his own design.

But all the strange madman meant was: a laser had come from the future and exploded on his retina. He could not have said it like so, but, this laser carried not photons but a single synchron, which did not collapse but instead spread over all the superimpositions of his mind.

It caused him to dream – not the dreams of normal men, but dreams in which his sight was restored; not just restored, but improved, to see that which no mortal eyes could see. In one dream he received a visit from a god who brought to him a mask. By the black snout, the long ears, there was no mistaking the god who brought it, for such was the face of Set, the foreign god, the slave god. The mask he brought was a helmet like none ever before seen. When the blind madman awoke he found that he had fashioned this mask, in his sleep, just as Set had presented it to him. He could not see this work he had made. But he could feel upon it where he had engraved a symbol: the Eye of the god who had brought it.

He did not use the mask himself, but buried it deep beneath the sand. Leave it here, Set told him, and in the necessary time the gods would find the gift that he had offered.

Monday morning, Will woke from a very strange and vivid dream. He was pretty sure it was his own voice that had roused him; it was still an hour before the alarm. He had been shouting for help, he thought, but why? It had not seemed like a nightmare. He tried to reconstruct it in his mind, but the details were already fading.

Something to do with his job, he thought. He remembered Pastor Drew being unhappy about something. Will couldn't make sense of it while awake. Somehow it had to do with picture frames, he thought, frames that people wore so they could fit inside other pictures. Pastor Drew was complaining about a frame in his office, one that didn't match the décor. Frames had to match the décor, Pastor Drew had said in the dream. He could see Pastor Drew's face, frowning, saying, "That's what frames are for."

Later in the dream, Will had felt a gnawing sense of wicked mischievousness, like an evil twin was taking over. For some reason – knowing he shouldn't – he had hidden one of the parishioners, Bailey Evans, in a closet. It was not a big deal, he had laughed in the dream.

But when he had opened the closet door, Bailey Evans had changed... He had grown the body of a bull, and his eyes had become angry and wild.

"Help!" Will had cried. "Help!"

But he woke up unafraid – instead with a dark, tense excitement. The mischievous twin still remained. He tried to shake it off and go back to sleep, but it wouldn't let go. Certain images gnawed at him: Pastor Drew's expression – his intent and earnest concern;

the face of Bailey Evans before he entered the closet –
confused, willing, innocent; his face when he came out
– the anger of the Minotaur. These particulars seemed
connected. He felt there was something the dream was
trying to tell him. Why Bailey Evans? What did that
mean? He didn't know. He couldn't get back to sleep,
but as much as he thought on the dream, it never
made any sense.

He grinned as he lay there, though he did not realize
it. He grinned a fierce and unapproachable grin, the
grin of his mischievous twin that he refused to
acknowledge. The grin remained until the alarm clock
wiped it away, and he started another day.

Monday.

All Duane could think about that day was the game
that night. Then it came, and he couldn't concentrate.
Was it the pressure? He tried not to think about it. But
the games were different now. Everybody was amped
up. Usually his edge was concentration, slipping
deeper into the moment than everybody else did. But
now he could see they all had it. They were all one with
the moment. He'd lost his edge.

It's okay, he told himself. Stay aggressive.

He put together a crossover and a spin to beat two
guys off the dribble, but the easy layup at the end

rolled out. He heard the excited shouts of the crowd, and the frustration brought a rush of adrenaline. But he wanted the challenge of the road; he loved it. He snatched the rebound out of the air, put it back up soft, missed again. This time it got knocked out of bounds by Leroy, the Las Vegas center.

Again the crowd went wild. He grimaced. Two misses right at the rim. He glanced over at coach. Frowning at him. He couldn't believe it. Concentrate!

And get back on defense.

Coach was shaking his head side to side. But as Dimes ran by he heard him shout: "Don't worry about it, Duane, good effort, good effort. Keep up the hustle!"

Duane tried to maintain focus. Defense. His man, Tyler, was a quick and clever ballhandler. Hard to keep up with. Duane gave him a little space, knowing he wasn't a great shooter. Play smart, he told himself.

And Tyler shot over him, Duane reaching for the ball, almost blocked it. Other hand in Tyler's eyes.

Swish. Crowd on their feet.

Nothing going right.

It's okay, Duane told himself. Concentrate. Stay in the moment.

Then, in the locker room between the third and the fourth quarter, talking to his teammate Chris, he felt something change. It was a shift in mood; Chris said something, Duane didn't know if he meant it to be rude. At first, he was standing by his locker alone, thinking about how disconnected he felt. Like he wasn't a part of anything. Why couldn't he focus? It was like everyone was in a different space than he was, or a different time, like they were all ghosts moving around doing their haunted thing. Leftover spirits of something that had already happened. They weren't tangible in a way he could interact with or interfere. So disconnected that he almost felt he could see through them. They were translucent. He stood by the locker, holding his towel, thinking these things, not realizing he was slowly turning in a circle, inspecting his teammates one by one, until finally they came to rest on Chris, the point guard – so fast they called him Lightning in the press. But in the locker room they called him Believer, his heart was so big. He was a little guy, a foot shorter, a hundred pounds lighter than was Duane. There was nothing ghostly about the eyes of Chris – clear and alive, smiling like he had just been told a joke. Or he was thinking of one, about to tell it – and that's what Duane thought when he opened his mouth, but what he said was, "Give me your towel, rook. I'm sweating bullets over here." Duane threw him his towel, even though Chris was sitting on his own. Chris wiped his face, breathed a deep sigh, threw it back soggy. "Stinkin' it up tonight, man," he said. "Make some shots this quarter."

That was all. It offended Duane at first, just for a second. But when Chris walked away, the air shifted and now Duane was looking at his teammates not as ghosts, but as animals alive and breathing. Not even men, but organisms of blood and tissue, sniffing for predators and prey, flaunting this and marking that, breathing oxygen and expelling carbon dioxide. Duane could smell them, and he realized suddenly, I am an animal among animals. I will show them my dominance, he thought, hardening to the minor insult, losing all emotion. Ferocious, his father had called him, ten years old. One-on-one, before they ever called him Dimes, he had been Ferocious.

It became simple then, in the fourth quarter. He heard their calls and cries and responded like an animal would, with immediacy and savagery. It wasn't anger. It was just he had realized it was right to do it. Tyler tried a hesitation move, Duane reached out and took the ball. The look of surprise on Tyler's face meant nothing to him. He barely saw it as he charged to the other side. Chris was already there, hand high, waiting for the ball, but Duane ignored him, too. He wasn't Dimes, he was Ferocious, pack-leader and first to feed. It was his trophy and he took it all the way to the peak one-handed. He looked at Chris and Chris was grinning – Chris had seen it coming, this change, some part of him said. Didn't matter.

The crowd was silent. Eighteen thousand animals, a pack as large as any gathered, wanting to scream their dominance like they had earned something. For shame, he told them silently, and they quietly bowed their heads.

He had already returned to Tyler, receiving the ball from the baseline. Give it to me, he thought, give me my prize. Tyler looked at him like he had never seen him before. He hadn't. Dimes was gone. And Ferocious grinned, hungry.

He could smell Tyler's fear.

"**Y**ou're not going to finish watching this?" Ben said. Gary had evacuated his space on the small dorm sofa and looked stressed as he stuffed notebooks into his bag.

"I need to meet with Dr. Evians," he said.

"Again?"

"He wants to pick up where we left off last night. We can run a lot more tests without having to recalibrate everything."

"You're going to miss something good," Ben said. "I can feel it. Look at Dimes' face. Something's different."

"I started recording it a second ago," Gary said, "right before the fourth quarter started." He watched Dimes steal the ball and run down the court for a dunk. "He does look different," he said. "He looks mean."

"I know!" Ben sounded proud of it.

"I wonder what set him off," Gary said. But he didn't have time to think about it. He was already running late. Seemed like he was always running late, he thought. If only he had a time machine.

"Are you recording over the last game?" Ben said, just as Gary was walking out the door.

"Yes."

Ben looked disappointed. "I wanted to keep them all. If they went all the way? That would be crazy."

"I'm late," Gary said, and left.

Dr. Evians was ecstatic when they examined the results. They had picked up a slight but clear trace of green in the light spectrum. "It's proved," he said. "I've proven it." A modest man, still he couldn't help feeling a bit puffed up by the moment.

Gary, too, was thrilled. "When are we going to present it?"

Dr. Evians came back to earth. "It should be properly presented in a paper, first." He patted Gary on the shoulder. "You'll be a co-author, of course. It's ours."

Gary said, "I'd love to do some more tests on the intensity level anomalies we measured last night. I think those may be indications of the wormhole activity I've theorized."

Evians smiled indulgently. "In good time," he said. "First let's get a team in here to duplicate what we've done. Meanwhile, we have a hefty paper to put together. There should be no problem working it out as your project grade. We'll work on it together, the two of us. I can tell you already you'll be receiving a very high mark. Your work up to this point has been excellent. More than excellent! We've proven it! The same results as yesterday. Verifiable, repeatable, predictable." He yawned leisurely, his head rolling back like a cat without a care. "Go home, Gary," he said. "We're done here. Let's meet in my office tomorrow and start drafting an outline."

"Sure," said Gary. He couldn't help whistling as he walked back to the dorm. He wanted to tell Ben he had discovered synchrons. Ben was nowhere to be found. Instead he watched the fourth quarter of the game. Disappointing - Highrollers lost by two. Down two games. Doubtful they could come back, but anything was possible.

Anything is possible, Gary repeated to himself. I've discovered synchrons. Shed a little light on a bit more of the void.

Not to mention, he thought – guilty and euphoric at the same time – one step closer to my Time Traveler.

Evians knocked on his daughter Kristen's door quietly, expecting silence, but after a moment he heard a sleepy, "Come in?" He opened the door to darkness. Now there were no invisible cobwebs of resistance – his mind was on other things.

"Kristen?"

"Hey, Daddy."

"I discovered a new particle."

"That's great, Dad. Tell me about it in the morning?"

"Okay," Evians said. Then, "I'm a genius."

"I know," she said. "You're the smartest Dad in the world." She meant it. He could hear it in her voice.

"Goodnight, pumpkin," he said, closing the door.

PART THREE

Fruit of the Fountain

Long did Seth, son of Adam, travel the great way in search of the Garden of Eden. He had nothing to guide him but the words of his father and the evidence of passage this first family had left behind, a millennia of ghostly memory: here Seth found the great stone beside which he had claimed his bride; here Seth found the altar upon which he had sacrificed his first hunt to the Lord; here was the pasture where he had first broken a stallion; here was the farm where he had been born, where his brothers had fought, one dead, one banished; here were the memories his father had tried to flee for a thousand years.

And here, finally, was the great Gate before the Garden. At the entrance, as his father had warned him, the Angel Gabriel stood, a mighty figure of light, two hands resting on the pommel of a sword of flame that rose a hundred feet high. Its point was thrust into the earth deep enough that the blade became a wall of fire through which there could be no passage.

The great eye of Gabriel looked down on the tiny man. His giant lips curled, his massive brow furrowed, but he said nothing, merely watched as Seth approached. He was a figure of the greatest light and majesty, clothed in robes of glory such as Seth had never seen.

"I am Adam's son," Seth said to the Angel, despite his fear. He shouted up to the face of judgment. "I have been sent for seeds from the Tree of Life."

For a moment he could not be sure if Gabriel heard him, but then the angel nodded deeply and moved the sword aside. "I have been waiting," he said, his voice like the thunder of a thousand storms, "for the son of Adam to return."

And Seth passed through the gate, the first man to do so in a thousand years.

Monday night, when Rick called, Will was watching *Moonstruck*. He wasn't much of a Cher fan, but he liked Nicolas Cage. He had seen it before; he remembered it funnier, had forgotten the sappy stuff, and now he felt a little goofy, by himself, sprawled on his bed, watching a romance, when he had thought he was merely committing to a comedy. He was now regretting it; dramas made him moody.

"Will," said Rick, on the phone, "are you busy?"

"Not really," said Will. "Watching a movie."

"I'm using the Eye of Set tonight," Rick said. "You want a turn?"

"I thought you said it was the Eye of Horus?"

"That's how I originally translated it," Rick said, "but I talked to an ancient scribe who had some texts I'd never seen... Probably lost. It described a mask that Set wore to make his journeys from the darkness into the light. So it *did* once belong to Set. It wasn't until after Set ripped out Horus' eye that Horus stole the mask to replace his missing sight. At least according to the papyrus the scribe had. After the two made peace, Set never challenged Horus' ownership of the Eye, so it's been the Eye of Horus ever since. But originally, before all that, it was most likely inscribed with the Eye of Set." Rick was more energized than usual, his words practically tumbling over one another in his enthusiasm to get them out.

"You've been using it? What about the Shadow?"

"No sign of it the last few times," said Rick. So he had been using it quite a bit. "You coming? I'm at the cabin, but I'm not going to be up all night."

"I'm on my way," said Will.

After he hung up, he got up to turn off the TV, but stopped, struck by the dialogue between Olympia Dukakis and Danny Aiello.

"There's a Bible story," Danny was saying, "God took a rib from Adam and made Eve. Now maybe men chase women to get the rib back. When God took the rib, he left a big hole there, where there used to be something. And the women have that. Now maybe, just maybe, a man isn't complete as a man without a woman."

That's bull, thought Will. I'm complete. He wasn't sure why the thought bothered him.

Olympia Dukakis, on the TV, said, "But why would a man need more than one woman?"

"I don't know," Danny Aiello said, and Will admired the casual way he delivered the next line: "Maybe because he fears death."

Will shut off the TV, thinking, I don't fear death. My loneliness has nothing to do with fear. He hadn't acknowledged this loneliness to himself; he still didn't, really. His mind verbalized the thought but didn't listen; it passed so quickly he barely noticed.

But on the drive out to Rick's cabin, he couldn't stop wondering, do I struggle with death? An idle thought at first, but as he drove he circled it more and more aggressively. Of course he struggled with death – he had told Rick, we want to know what it all means. We don't want to die before we know what it means. Was that true? Was he afraid of it? He didn't fear the pain, or the suffering, if such things were a part. He didn't really believe in hell, an eternal damnation, nor in heaven the way it was described. But he believed in spiritual continuance, a life beyond, an opening of a door into a deeper understanding. He told himself, there is nothing to fear in the process of death.

But he was thinking.

Brooding.

Wondering.

What am I afraid of? Why do I struggle so? Something... his stomach churned, his breath came faster just imagining it, thinking about the real possibility of physical end. And now something else occurred to him: that by turning a single lens, he could see into the future. I could watch it happen, he told himself. I could *see* it. Couldn't I?

I could *stop* it, was his next thought. Turn the *other* lens, not the "potentiator," to use Rick's terms, but the "activator"... What Will thought of as the "travel knob." His heart was hammering. Why had he not thought of this before? Had Rick? He had never asked him.

Nor would he tell him what he planned. Rick wouldn't like it. Probably he wouldn't allow it. But the decision was already made in Will's mind – he would do it tonight, he told himself. Confront the fear – for there's nothing to fear. Look upon the struggle and see there was no struggle.

I will view my own death, he thought, as the speedometer, unnoticed, climbed higher.

Ben came into Gary's room and shook him awake, which was highly unusual. "Gary," he said urgently, "who won the game last night?"

"What?" said Gary, confused and irritated. "I gave you the tape."

"Yeah, I watched it," said Ben. "Who won?"

"Highrollers did, I think. Why?"

"Yes," said Ben, absurdly pleased, his face a grinning mask of glee. "They did." For a moment, Gary thought he would be let back to sleep, but then Ben said, "Come in here, you have to see this."

"I'm in my boxers," protested Gary. "What time is it?"

"I don't know. It's like two."

"In the morning?"

"Just get dressed and come see this."

"I already watched the game," said Gary.

"Just come on," Ben said, exiting through the divider. Gary contemplated going back to sleep, but after a second he groaned and pulled himself to a standing position.

Ben had put the tape in the VCR in front of the couch and the TV was paused on an image of Duane Dimes, grinning half-shyly at the camera while being interviewed. The score was shown at the bottom right, Las Vegas over Houston, 119-104.

"This is after the game. I just paused it," said Ben.

"Yeah, I watched this," said Gary.

"Okay, just watch it again."

Ben started the video and they heard the tail-end of the sidelines reporter asking a question about playing time. "It's work ethic," Dimes responded. "Work ethic leads to success. It gets you more playing time. Makes you more consistent on the floor. Coach knows I'm committed. Knows I'm committed to that."

"Yeah, I remember that," said Gary.

Ben paused the VCR again. "Now wait," he said, "and don't look away from the TV."

"Okay," Gary shrugged.

"I'm serious. Don't look away."

"Okay," Gary repeated, irritated.

Ben hit rewind, for only a second, and again they caught the tail end of the question about playing time. "It's all in your work ethic," Dimes said, "and commitment. It's how you approach the game. Commitment to what you're doing leads to success."

"Wait," said Gary. "That's not what he said before." His head was still a bit foggy from sleep. "Rewind that one more time."

"Okay," said Ben, again warning, "don't look away. Don't look away. Don't look away!"

"I got it," said Gary.

"It's commitment to the game," said Dimes. "Hustle, you know. I think... I try to stay committed to the moment, committed to what we're trying to achieve. You have to prepare hard, then you have to play hard. I try to do both, and Coach left me on the floor, gave me some opportunities."

"Hold on," said Gary. "I need some coffee."

As he brewed a cup, Ben said, "Do you remember how the game ended last night?"

"Yes," said Gary, adding some sugar. "Dimes took over early in the fourth when they were down three. I think he had sixteen in the fourth? Phenomenal."

"Yes," said Ben, grinning. "That's how it finally turned out. The first time, though, they lost big. Second was closer but still a loss. Third round, Dimes went off huge. Not too shabby!"

"What are you talking about?" said Gary.

"The tape," said Ben. "Gary, listen – you invented your time machine. I mean, sort of."

"What?"

"I don't know what you did to that tape, but every time you rewind it, every time, the game comes out different. Well, I think you have to be watching it," he amended. "When I rewound it the fast way it came out the same. Or at least it seemed like it did. Maybe I missed something."

"What?" repeated Gary.

"You know, like maybe things changed, but I wasn't *conscious* of it, see? I still have some experiments to do," said Ben. "Also, I have a few scientific questions, things I need to know, since you invented it. First, can you do it again?"

"What?" said Gary.

"I mean, like, make another one. And, if I record something over it, would *that* change, too? About how many times do you think you can record over something before it will wear out? Also, I know it's analog, it's magnetic tape, right? There's no way we could degrade the quality of the universe? I mean, its resolution – like, the integrity of time itself shouldn't be compromised, right? That's impossible. You know what I'm talking about? I hope that's impossible but I wasn't a hundred percent sure. Oh, and last question, if I copied an old tape onto it, I mean like a tape from the past, can I change history?"

"What?" said Gary, one more time.

"Well I'm not talking like, World War II videos or anything. I'm not stupid," Ben said. "It's just I've got some old home videos." He spread his hands apologetically, but his smirk was full of mischievous glee. "They could have come out better."

I will view my own death. Will had only that in his mind as he picked up the Artifact, but as he held it the thought was still shaded with questions and considerations, of his life, purpose and design, none of which rose fully to the surface. He did not realize his mind was still considering the movie, Danny Aiello's argument that men were unfulfilled by nature, a piece of the soul cut out and given to woman. Consciously, all he told himself was: "I will view my death." It sent a cold nervousness up his spine that made him hesitate. Noticing his odd mood, Rick frowned, his eyes narrowing. But before he could say anything, Will shook off the cold chill, slid the helmet over his head and felt everything change. It locked over his eyes, one blurry, the other crystal clear, looking at Rick, who regarded him with a frown.

With the Artifact over his head, Will felt the usual cold separation, as though he and Rick existed on different planes. He turned the right eye, blurring it like the other. Time has literally stopped, he thought.

What does death really even matter? It is my thought, my consciousness alone that owns this moment. He continued to rotate the lens ("Look before you leap," Rick constantly warned), the prospect of his own death firmly in mind, and the image slowly slid into focus, revealing a richly colored garden. Splashes of color resolved themselves into huge flowers, trees so bright they looked painted.

His first thought was that he had died in a research facility. This conclusion was drawn from the even, solid hue of the sky, the lack of sun, the pure uninterrupted ambience of the light. It seemed environmentally controlled, it was so clean and organized, with strange plants that looked made of wax. An alien botanic gardens.

But these thoughts were swept away the next instant when his eye focused, through the lens of the Artifact, on a hulking shape some distance from him. *The Shadow!* his mind screamed. But it was not that. The Shadow crept from the outside in, into both lenses. This, though like it – the same dark, moving blackness – was limited to the focused right lens. This, whatever it was, was alive: a being, some sort of creature silhouetted in Shadow. It sucked away the light, it seemed – but he could not look directly at it or the haze that surrounded it.

Instead he looked to the ground before it, where it

crouched over something, as though working. It was a figure lying on the ground, he realized – a naked man.

Is that me? he wondered. Do I die at the hands of this monster?

All this in the space of a breath. But then the hulking beast started to turn and at the same moment the true Shadow began creeping about the edges of his vision. His hands flew to his head of their own accord, his breath catching, but just before he ripped the helmet from his head he saw the face of the creature – blinding light, so bright it blotted out the Shadow. So bright it burned.

Then back at the cabin, holding the Artifact in his hands, sweating, heart hammering. He felt like he had been struck by lightning. Rick: "What are you doing?" He took the helmet from Will's trembling grasp. "I've told you to be careful. What have you done?"

"Nothing," Will said, having trouble catching his breath. "I didn't... I just looked, I didn't do anything."

"What was it?" Rick asked. He'd never asked before. "You've been standing there shaking for twenty minutes."

"I don't know," Will said. "I don't know what I saw."

Rick pulled him close, angry, looking intently in his eyes. "What were you thinking?"

"My death," Will confessed. He wasn't sure if that was the question. Rick's face was inscrutable, but he let go of Will's collar. He still gripped the Artifact with his other hand. Now he set it on the table gently. "I wanted to see how I died," Will said.

"You're a fool," Rick said.

"But I don't think that was me," Will said. He didn't want to tell Rick what he thought. Rick already thought he was a fool.

"I should never have shown you this," Rick said. "I thought you would be more responsible."

"I am responsible," Will objected.

"This is probably the greatest power the world has ever seen," said Rick. "I thought you understood that. I'm not even sure you should be using it."

"I'm not sure *you* should be using it," Will said, angry, unlike himself. But he was still unbalanced from the experience of the Artifact.

Rick looked taken aback. "It is *mine*," he said. "It was left to *me*."

"Well maybe it shouldn't have been," Will said.

Rick's eyes widened in surprise, then slowly his face turned to stone. "I have exchanged ideas with the greatest philosophers and scientists of all time," he said coldly. "I have explored the deepest crevices of history. I have argued with Plato and Newton. What mind has more right than mine?"

"*Everyone*," said Will, his wild heart still unsettled. He wasn't sure if he was angry or afraid. But he spoke to Rick in a way he never had before. "Anyone who wears it. You think it was meant for you alone? If that were the case it wouldn't *work* for anyone else, that's what *I* think." He thought of the Minotaur, the girls who had surely died, and other things, all a mass of swirling catalyst in his mind at once. "You think it was left to you for a purpose? But what purpose, Rick? So you can write another boring book on quantum mechanics? You're not even using it right." He shook his head, frustrated with himself, his anger, his inability to communicate. "I put it on and I have just as much power as you. I just don't know how to put it – like you, in physics, in math. But the things I've seen... I watched a boy named Arthur draw a sword from solid stone. I saw a hammer draw lightning in the hands of a giant man in Scandinavia. You say it's the most powerful thing in existence, but you haven't even tried to look into the future?"

"That's ridiculous," said Rick.

"Anyone could wear it," said Will. "Anyone."

"I don't believe you've ever seen these things," Rick said, his tone like he was speaking to a rebellious child. "Why lie about that?"

"Go look!" said Will, indicating the helmet. But Rick shook his head.

"Go home," he said. His voice was final, carrying resignation and disappointment, while his eyes were mad with angry fire.

Will left. He was already ashamed with himself, his furious outburst. He wanted to apologize. But he wasn't going to, because he knew deep down he was right. He just didn't know how Rick, despite all his intelligence, could fail to understand. I will have to show him, he thought. Just show him what I've seen.

After Will left, Rick put the Artifact back on his head. What could he possibly have seen that I haven't? he thought. He could not believe in fantasy – that Will had experienced anything beyond that which could be explained by reason. Mythology? Legends? These were the rationalizations of primitive cultures that lacked the capacity to scientifically explain the complex behaviors of more subtle systems. Given calculus, one need no other gods.

Take me to the sword in the stone, he told the helmet, a range of times and possibilities in mind. But when he turned the lens, what he saw was no British King of the Dark Ages, but instead a man in a studio, pencil in hand, sketching at an easel. Rick watched for a bit as the man drew a boy – thick, cartoonish strokes, Rick thought – standing before a brick wall, regarding an anvil, the barest outline of a sword already sketched above it. This is not real, Rick thought, this is a cartoon. What is this? And with no regard for caution or consequences he turned the other lens, actively entering the scene.

The man looked up from his drawing, shocked, but, as was the way of the Artifact, he recovered quickly, seeing whatever he needed to see for the purposes of the helmet. "Do you need something?" he asked Rick, looking a little irritated. "I'm in the middle of this."

"What are you doing?" Rick demanded.

The man's brow furrowed. "That's none of your business!" He pulled a cloth over the picture.

"It's just a story," said Rick. "A myth."

"A fairy tale," agreed the man. Or was he mocking him?

Rick turned the lens again, furious, thinking, Show me the *real* King Arthur. This was better, he thought. Now he was in a Medieval bed-chamber, a man before him stooped over a chamber pot, vomiting with a violence painful to watch, with wrenching motions that twisted his body into a fetal fist, spasms that made his hands white on the edges of the dirty pot. Rick could see tears streaming down his face, and the man's robe, a fine fur, hung loosely over his huddled form, drenched in sweat.

Rick turned the other lens, entering the scene, and hearing some sound, the retching King Arthur turned, wiping his bearded face with a soggy rag. "Leave me!"

148

"You are just a man," said Rick.

"And you," said Arthur. "You are a traitor and a coward." Then he shook his head and laughed grimly. "Well, no coward at that." And violent spasms turned him away for a moment. He turned back, snot crusting his moustache, bits of regurgitated food in his beard. "Leave me, or I will have your head." As he said it his hand reached for the hilt of a sword that lay by his side, a simple weapon with a curved, unadorned cross-guard and a pommel in the shape of a diamond, its long blade hidden within a fine leather scabbard.

Rick would have replied but the Shadow – no! he thought, no! I will see what I wish – but the Shadow crept into his vision and he had no choice but to pull the helmet from his head in fear.

After leaving Rick's, Will stopped by Dave's to drop off a DVD. He didn't want to – he was rattled and upset – but Dave only lived five minutes from Rick's cabin and now there was no telling when Rick would invite him back.

"This one is a continuation of last week's series," he told Dave, handing him a DVD and repeating what Pastor Drew had asked for. "It's just the clip at the end. Last thirty seconds, with the tornado approaching and everybody looking scared. There's a quote he wants

149

after it, from Job."

"He e-mailed it to me," said Dave. "I said it would be fine. I've already got it rendering. If you wait a few minutes I can give it to you now."

"Sure," said Will, and, as always, began looking over Dave's table of gadgets. "What's that?" he said, pointing at one.

"You can touch them, Will, it's not like this is a museum."

"Sure," said Will, "but I bet some of this is expensive." He picked up a thin device from where it sat atop a small Roland keyboard.

"That is the Elite SlimCam USB from Sony," Dave said. "HD recording compressed in a tiny mpeg format."

"This is a video recorder?" echoed Will, looking at the tiny device.

"I know," said Dave, grinning. "It's really a spy cam, but they advertise it as home security." He wheeled over to a filing cabinet on the other side of the room and shuffled through one of the drawers, finally pulling out a little strap. "Here, hand it over." Will gave it to him and he attached it to the strap, then wrapped both around his head. The camera fit snugly over one eye. "Hold on, I've got to turn it on first." He took it off, pressed a button on the camera, and slid the whole thing back on his head. "There," he said. "Perfect."

"Looks like a monocle," said Will. It was tiny. It would fit in the Artifact, he thought. Would it record it? Could that be done? There was a reason he had come to Dave's tonight, he thought; this must be it.

"Sometimes I wear it on my head when I'm working on stuff," Dave said, "to keep track of what I'm doing. That way I can be creative while I work and still go back and fix anything I break."

"Nice," said Will. "That's a very good idea." Then, "Where can I get one of these? How much are we talking?"

"It's not too bad," said Dave. "Like three fifty. But, hey, you want to try that out a little bit? I don't mind if you borrow it."

"Really?" said Will. "It is pretty cool."

"You'll love it. Just don't do anything I wouldn't do."

"Of course not," Will said. "Do you have time to show me how it works?"

Rick had just put the Artifact away when Will returned. "No," said Rick. He was, if anything, angrier than when Will had left. "You're not touching it. And certainly not with that thing on your head. I think we need to take some time off. If you use it too much it increases the density of the synchronic effect. It has to have time to discharge."

"That's techno-babble."

"How long was it, the last time, before you saw the shadow?" Rick said it as casually as he could; He could see it still made Will shudder. It was difficult for Rick as well, only minutes removed from the Shadow's presence, but he controlled his voice tightly, not wanting Will to see how deeply he was disturbed.

"Not very long," Will admitted. He had apologized for earlier, and while Rick was still angry, in truth he was willing to bend. Still frustrated by his failures just moments ago – which he had not mentioned to Will – he was more than willing, almost looking for an excuse to let himself be talked into it. The Shadow be damned. So when Will said, "*You* test it," Rick unbent enough to take the camera from his hand.

"You think it doesn't really show history," he said. "You think it's like a dream. A magnificent hallucination." He fiddled with the camera for a moment, powering it on, quickly finding the button that began it recording. It had no LCD screen, just a blinking red light and the camera lens. "You think it amplifies imagination. How could you see gods and legends if not so? But I don't *believe* you, Will." He fiddled with the camera, figuring it out easily. Will watched as he started it recording and slipped it over his head, the monocle effect making him look like a mad cyborg doctor with a mechanical eye.

"I don't know what it does," said Will. "Maybe those things are real."

Rick picked up the Artifact and held it for a moment. "I will teach you how to use it. Focus your mind on this moment." He looked at the clock. "It is now eight-oh-nine p.m. It is dates and times that are important, Will. This is how you see history instead of imagination."

He put the Artifact on his head. The camera was uncomfortable for a moment, then, when the Artifact settled onto his shoulders, he ceased to notice it. Was the camera still recording? Was it even still there? He couldn't be sure. It had partially blocked his vision before. Now he could clearly see with both eyes; Will still before him on one side, but the other eye, the left, blurred and out of focus. The camera was on the right.

The Artifact was blissful peace. The Artifact erased his worries. The Artifact was power. He looked at the clock – now eight-ten – and he waited, waited, until it turned again – eight-eleven, and then he thought about eight-oh-nine and slowly, ever so slowly, turned the right lens. And there he was before himself, fiddling with the camera.

It was just as it had been, everything exactly as had occurred two minutes ago, he thought. Of course it was. He had no question about the Artifact's historical accuracy. He had used it a thousand times. He watched himself say, "But I don't *believe* you, Will," and start the camera recording.

But then, to his surprise, the other Rick handed Will the camera. This was not right, he thought, as Will put the camera over his eye. This is not what happened, The peace of the Artifact faded, a dissonant anxiousness left in its wake. He reached up to his left eye but hesitated... he had never intruded on his own self before.

The other Rick took the Artifact from the table and put it into Will's hands. No, thought, Rick, why are you doing that? Don't you realize Will is naïve and dangerous? But Will slid the Artifact onto his head and now they were both wearing one. Impossible, thought Rick. I have to stop this. But the moment he touched the left lens Will turned his head and they were looking at each other. Will's face, like Rick's own, was hidden behind the golden gleam of the mask; but for the rest of Will – his shirt, his jeans, his slouch – it could have been anyone inside the Artifact. As Rick's fingers rested on the left lens of his own helmet, Will's rested similarly on the right.

And then, as though connected, both started to turn, of their own volition.

Will was as frightened as Rick to see him standing there. Two Ricks in the same room. But he was even more frightened when the lens moved, all on its own, under his fingers. His eyes blurred and his stomach rolled over and he realized the Artifact was carrying him somewhere. This time there was not even the illusion of control.

He thought – not by choice, but in panic – of the creature he had seen, the beast of light and shadow hunched over the man in the garden.

Then his eyes came into focus.

A garden? thought Rick, as splashes of color resolved themselves into trees and flowers too bright to be natural. Plastic, he thought. He was in a pasture. He tried to turn around, to look behind him, but he found to his dismay he couldn't move. It took him a moment to realize it – there was always dissociation while wearing the Artifact – but he came to discover he had no sensation, no feeling in his body, his arms, his legs.

He was trapped, he thought. The Artifact had never trapped him before. Always he had moved as a man, experienced sensation as a man. Now, he could feel only the vaguest of impressions. Warmth. The sun was behind him; he felt its heat beating down. His mind feared; his mind panicked. But there was no reflection in his body: no hammering heart, no shortness of breath. Just the warmth of the sun and the sights and sounds of the garden.

Through the trees Will saw two figures move, but he could not follow them, trapped as he was. They were people – man and woman. They arrived together and stopped far off. With the sun in his eyes he could not see them clearly. He thought they were looking at him, though they didn't come near. Their skin was dark like clay and unmarked in any way. Their hair was long and uncombed. They wore no clothes or jewelry.

Adam and Eve, he thought.

Rick stared at the woman; he could not help it. There was something in the way she stood, a natural grace, a sensual beauty. She looked wild, he thought, like an untamed animal. But she looked at him with a brightness in her eyes that scattered his thoughts.

He looked at the man, too, the eyes equally bright. Studying Rick intently. Holding hands with the woman as they talked. The tilt of the man's head spoke of amusement. He appeared to tug at the woman's hand, and they wandered off.

Primitives, Rick thought. Prehistoric savages.

She came back alone, much later, and he called out to her. "Please!" he said. "Help me!" She stopped, a startled look on her face, and instead of passing by as it seemed she had intended, she stopped and peered into his face.

"You speak names," she said, amazed.

"Free me," he said, equally amazed this savage could understand. "I'm trapped."

"Trapped," she repeated, like it was a word she had never heard before, and she ran away. He remained, unmoving, barely feeling. As night came he drifted off into what seemed like sleep, a long drift of wind empty of conscious thought that lasted well into the morning. When he awoke the world had returned to its preternatural brightness.

In the afternoon he saw the woman talking to her mate again. In the distance the man's face was inscrutable as the woman paced and gestured with excitement. The man went away. The woman approached him.

"How does a tree speak names?" she wondered. "None of the other trees speak names." She looked around, a look of concern crossing her face. "How does a tree have mouths and speak?"

"I'm not a tree," said Rick. "I'm a man."

"You are named Tree," said the woman, confidently; then, her mood shifting abruptly, her tone becoming quiet, "We have been forbidden to taste of your fruit." She looked up at him, her unkempt hair shading her eyes, making no attempt to hide her nakedness.

"Listen to me," said Rick, "I'm stuck here. You have to remove this helmet from my head." He tried to indicate but felt nothing, no response from limb or nerve.

"I do not know these names," she said. "Adam has never said these names to me."

"I need to go home," said Rick, desperate.

"Home," she repeated, her eyes widening. "Home," she said again, exploring the sound of it. "What is home?"

"It's where I came from." It was like speaking to a child, he thought. What was the point? "Have you no mother, no father?"

"Mother. Father. Home," she repeated, like a dull student. But she didn't appear stupid. Her animated eyes searched his face. "What does this mean? Mother?"

Rick said, "The woman who gave birth to me." Her eyebrows furrowed, confused. "The woman who made me," he persisted.

Her face became still, her mouth making a little circle. Thinking. Then: "How does a woman make a tree?"

"I'm not a tree," he insisted. "I'm a man."

Her mouth pursed, her eyes became rounder. "How does a woman make a man," she said, "to become a mother?" Her voice was hushed. "She makes him from mud?"

"I'm not supposed to be here," said Rick. "Please, just take the helmet from my head. Please?"

"Helmet?" she said. "Hel-met." Sounding each syllable.

"From my face," he said. "My head."

"The fruit?" she said, reaching toward him, slowly, her hand hovering by his face. "I mustn't touch the fruit." But still her hand came forward, so that for a moment he thought she was going to remove the Artifact. But she encountered no resistance from the mask; instead her fingers brushed his face, the consequences of that touch strange and unexpected: immediately, for just one moment, he felt the entirety of his body again, his feet planted firmly on the ground, her hand touching his face. He felt grass under his feet, and looked down, realizing he was naked. He was aroused, also, to his shame. He had not realized it. Their bodies were close together, her scent overwhelming in that instant.

Her eyes flicked down with his, widened. Her hand went from his face down, grasped him. "You are a man," she said, in wonder, and in that moment, freed from restraint, Rick reached up to tear the Artifact from his head.

Seth came to where a tree stood alone in the garden. It was not the Tree of Life, not that which he sought, but when it called out to him, he came near, and Seth saw that this tree was the Tree of Man.

"Please!" said the tree. "You must free me."

So Seth, having pity on it, took the mask that bound it and the tree went silent. Then he went to the Tree of Life and found there the seeds he was looking for. On his way out of the garden, he found the guardian of the Gate had changed.

"I am Michael," the giant told Seth, "the Lord of the Way."

"May I take this from the Garden?" he asked. He had not put it on, but he admired its beauty. "The Tree of Man begged that I free it from its burden."

"Take it," said Gabriel. "We give it unto you, for you have been chosen that the way will be known to those who seek the light."

Seth left the Garden carrying the mask under one arm and the seeds of Life in one hand. He was too late for Adam; he found his father's body just after it had expelled its last breath, still undisturbed by the decay of the earth.

Seth did as his father had asked him and placed the seeds of Life in his mouth. Then he buried Adam's body at the top of the hill, where it was watered first by his tears, and later by the tears of generations of his sons.

After grieving, Seth took up the mask and the inheritance of the cruel and unforgiving earth, and placed the burden of man upon his head.

When Rick pulled the Artifact away, his stomach wrenched, his vision blurred, and then he was standing back in the cabin. He was fully clothed. Except for the clarity of his memory, the scene in the garden might never have happened. Before him stood Will, the camera attached to his head. Rick's own head had no adornment: no helmet, no monocle-like recording device. His hands fell to his side, empty.

They stared at each other for a moment. Will looked scared, slightly manic. He said, "I lost it. I lost the Artifact," then, "I'm sorry. I couldn't control it."

Rick said nothing. I've had it wrong all along, he was thinking. It was never me, he thought. Will was right. It was always the helmet.

"I had no choice. I had to let him take it," Will said. "I was trapped."

Rick nodded. "It's okay," he tried to say, but only succeeded in clearing his throat awkwardly. He put his hand on Will's shoulder, calming him. "It's fine," he said. When Will had relaxed a little, he said, "Are you all right?"

"There's no Artifact," Will said. "It's gone."

"It's okay," Rick said again. They were words he wasn't used to forming. But he said them one more time: "It's okay, Will." Then, "Do you want to see what you got on the camera?"

Will took it from his head and looked at it. It turned out the battery was dead.

Gary ejected the VCR tape from the recorder. It was a tape that rewinds time, he thought. I invented my time machine.

But he didn't feel good about it. Thinking about possible consequences had kept him awake all night. He had watched the Duane Dimes interview a few more times, then stopped, thinking, what else am I affecting? What else happened in those ninety seconds, that minute and a half I just erased and started again? He did it one more time, letting memory wash over him like waves, looking for a shift, a change, something that would indicate a fragmentation, a break in the continuity of the world.

But he wouldn't know, would he? Not just from this. On this tape, it was just a game. Just an inconsequential sporting event.

What if it had been an election?

What if it had been a war?

He carried the tape outside and stomped on it, breaking it into tiny pieces. Ben's going to be pretty upset with me, he thought, his plans for the Highrollers championship destroyed.

But I made it, Gary thought. It's mine to do what I choose.

He leaned down and picked up the black magnetic strip, pulling it and tearing it as much as possible. On the way back inside, he dropped it all in the wastebasket at the door of the building.

I just don't think we're ready for this sort of thing, he thought.

Eve ran back to Adam with a strange fire inside of her, and when he saw her, he knew something had changed.

"What have you done?" he said. He was not angry with her – he didn't even know what such a thing might mean. Nor was he afraid, for he had never had anything to fear. Still, he frowned without knowing why, at a question, a doubt, a realization she had caused consequences without his awareness.

This worry was revealed in his face, but Eve didn't see it. Her eyes were drawn away, down to where a serpent curled at his stomach, whispering to her. A wonder, she thought, that she had never noticed its voice before. But now she grabbed for it, held it. And the fruit of Adam ripened in her hand.

So you've proven everything is connected?" Kristen asked, taking her dad's cereal bowl and rinsing it in the sink. She put it in the dishwasher with the other dirty dishes and started its cycle.

"No," Henry said, "I didn't say *that*, I just said we've proven synchrons."

"Right. But you've told me before they connect everything."

"Everything was already connected," Henry said. "The universe is a system."

"And you've proven that the system is all connected by synchrons. You even *once* said that it was all connected to *one* synchron."

"Well we've only proven they exist," he said, thinking, have I really said all those things? He had to remember not to speculate out loud in front of others.

"How big is a synchron?" she said.

Henry paused, trying to do some rapid math in his head without success. "We haven't measured its *size*."

"*Could* one be that big?" she said. "The size of the universe?"

"Of course not," he said. "The universe is infinite."

"Did you prove that?" she said, excited.

"No."

"Disappointing," she said. "That would be *really* big. But still, proving everything is connected... that's pretty earth-shattering, right?"

"I didn't prove that," said Henry, again. "We just proved synchrons."

"Who is this student, the one who gave you the idea?"

"Gary," said Henry. "Gary Dermont. He's a good kid. He reminds me of myself at his age." He shook his head, burdened with sudden thoughts of his failures and his weaknesses. "It seems like he worries too much."

"Yeah. Sounds like you," Kristen said.

"*He* thinks we've proved time travel," he chuckled. "Good kid."

Kristen started the dishwasher and kissed him on the cheek. "I got to go to school. I'll be late. Don't you have a morning class?"

He did. He hadn't forgotten about it, but he had lost track of the time. He got up quickly; wouldn't do to be later than his students. Had to set a good example, he thought. It's all you can do for them.

"I'll be home late," Kristen said. "I'm tutoring a girl in calculus after school."

"Be careful," Henry said. He almost said something else. Almost said a thousand things.

"Of course," she said. "It's just calculus."

Should we wait?" said Will, as the camera charged, "Or do you want to know what I saw?"

"You can tell me," said Rick.

"Okay," Will said, taking a moment to gather his thoughts. He slowly sank into the lone chair in the room, his shoulders slumped, his chin sinking to his chest. "First, I saw you," said Will. "At least, I think it was you, it was your sweater." He frowned. "The one you're wearing now."

"What was I doing?" asked Rick.

"You were here in the room, in front of the table. You were wearing the Artifact." They both looked at the empty table. "Then I don't know what happened. I was turning the... what do you call it? The potentiator? But I never *touched* the... the activator." These were technical names Rick had given to the eyepieces, words he had used when he had first shown Will the helmet.

"Go on," said Rick.

"I was thinking of the time," Will said, "Eight-oh-nine pm, just like you said. And then I saw you wearing the Artifact. And then I was in the Garden of Eden." He clutched his head. "I know you don't believe that. But it turned on its own. Did you see it? I know I didn't touch it."

"You didn't touch it," said Rick. "How do you know it was the Garden of Eden?"

"You'll see it in the recording," Will said, defensive. "I hope. How long does it take it to charge, do you think?"

Rick shrugged, then asked, "Did you see Adam and Eve?"

Will set his jaw as though expecting Rick to argue. "Yes." His look was challenging. "Yes I did."

"Did you see God?"

"No," Will said. He swallowed. "I was trapped. I think I was inside a tree." He looked crestfallen for a moment, then, in a low tone, a tone of deep depression, a tone Rick had never heard from Will before, he said: "I was there so long, Rick. So long." And he started to cry. Rick himself felt no desire to weep, but he felt a great weight in the pit of his stomach, and he realized it wasn't for his own self – it was compassion for his friend. He patted Will's arm awkwardly. Will glanced up into his eyes, embarrassed, but when he saw Rick's face he gained some composure. He sat up, wiping at his face. For a moment his eyes took on a distant look, remembering. "They never spoke to me," he said. "I could see them talking but they never... I don't think they noticed me. Then they were gone," he said. "She was crying, the woman. Eve," he repeated again, a defiant glint in his eye. "Eve was crying. The man –

Adam – he was comforting her. And then they were gone." Tears started leaking from his eyes again, slow tears that it seemed he didn't notice. "Then there was no one." He looked at Rick with a reflection of the raw, desperate loneliness he had felt.

"It's good that it's gone," said Rick, seeing that Will was having difficulty continuing. "The Artifact was... more than we were meant for."

He took the camera, still plugged into the computer, and turned it on. It was still working. It had just enough power to erase the video file and format the video card.

"What are you doing?" said Will. He got up and looked over Rick's shoulder. "I need to show you the video... I need to prove... We need to know what it means."

"We don't need to," said Rick. "I believe you." And then, with an unusual peace, a complacence new to him, "We'll never know what it means." He handed the empty recorder to Will. "I was wrong," he said. "The experiment proved, if anything, what you thought it would."

"I don't even know what I was trying to prove," said Will.

"That some things are beyond me. Beyond us."

"Okay," said Will. "I guess I was."

"The appearance of the Artifact... and its

disappearance. Both are mysteries we were never meant to understand."

Seth buried his father Adam atop a great hill. From afar it appeared to have the shape of a rounded brow – the head of the skull. In the earliest recorded histories it was told that this hill truly was the skull of Adam, the buried forefather of men, from long ago when they had walked the earth as giants.

At the top of this Skull grew a tree, sprung from the Seeds of Life. Seth cared for the tree until his death. With the use of his mask, gifted by the Angel Michael, Seth even cared for the tree after his death, thousands of years, until shadow blocked the path of light and he could see no farther into that future.

He performed many other acts of service in many places under many guises. Despite his best intentions, he also performed acts of incredible destruction, and these too have been recorded in the legends and histories of man.

This was the monstrous burden of Seth; this was his legacy, a struggle he inherited from the sins of his father. He was neither Cain nor Abel, but the third son; from birth he had known both the gift and the guilt of mankind.

Richard read what he had written of his book, all in one sitting, and sat back shaking his head. It was fragmented, it lacked coherence. And it was flawed from the very foundation, he thought. The premise is untenable; the hypothesis has been disproved.

But there were many good passages, many excellent observations.

Perhaps if he struck out all the things he now knew to be wrong, all his false assumptions, his forced conclusions, he could find the meaning of it. Discover what made it significant.

He began immediately, diving into the work, attempting a transformation. But his office – usually his haven – stifled him. It was too dark, too crowded with books, projects, papers. He couldn't think.

Suddenly he needed sunlight, fresh air. Now I know I'm a tree, he joked to himself. So he went out to the campus green with his laptop and a notebook. All the benches were taken by students, who were everywhere enjoying the beautiful day. He realized with a yearning regret how long he had resented them their pleasure. He sat on the grass, thinking, reading, taking notes.

He became lost in it, for how long he didn't know. Then a voice interrupted him: "I've never seen you working out here." He looked up at Rachel, the new Rachel – the only Rachel, now, he thought – not surprised at her appearance. Pleased. Wasn't that the reason he had come out here? "I haven't seen you smile like that before, either," said Rachel, a funny skepticism to her tone. "Work must be going well."

"It's terrible," he said. "But I think it can be fixed."

"That's good, then." She didn't walk off right away or sit down and join him, but stood there, looking down, clutching her book and her purse tightly to her side, frowning indecisively.

"I've come to conclude," he said, "that love... it's not just for survival." She didn't say anything. "Maybe it's like you say. To teach us compassion."

"I don't know if I really believe that," she said.

"Or to teach us something even beyond compassion. Something else altogether."

"Something else?"

"Something deeper." As the morning had worn on the day had become hotter and the green had become less crowded; now, there were only a few people in the park. Many of the benches were empty. Rick closed his laptop and his notebook, folding both under an arm. As he began to stand, Rachel offered him a hand. He took it and she helped him to his feet. "I'm working on my book," he said. "But it needs work."

"Yes?" she said guardedly. She let go of his hand, but they remained very close to each other; he thought passingly how odd it was that they seemed to seek

171

each other's space, then put up barriers when they were within it.

"I think it could use perspective," he said. "Would you like to help?"

She frowned, stepping back, looking him over critically. "Why are you saying that?" He didn't understand why she had become defensive. She said, "You don't share your work. You're famous for it."

He had not realized that. "People talk about that?" he said. "That I won't share my work?"

She looked perplexed. "You're well known for your secrecy."

"Yes," he said.

"So why are you toying with me?" she said. He didn't know what she meant. He frowned, trying to figure it out, but her face grew tight in the meantime, and she finally said, "I'm twenty-eight years old. I know what I am and I know what I'm not. You don't need to impress me with your book. You're Dr. Richard Mayliss." She returned again the step she had retreated. "Are you deliberately cruel? Or are you not the brilliant man they say you are?"

"I'm not," he said. "Either of those things."

"Obviously," she said, a barb, a parry and riposte, and he thought, why couldn't they get it right? Why couldn't they say with words what was clear in the exchange of eyes, the movement of bodies?

"When we first met," he said, "you asked me my favorite number."

"I remember," she said. "Phi. The golden ratio."

"I devoted a chapter to it. I think it's the best chapter in the book. I don't know why I put it in." He shrugged. "I think that's why it's the best one – because it was a mystery, even to myself. I had never thought about it, my favorite number. But they have meaning."

"Yes," she said. "They do."

"Before, I thought they were just measurements." I spoke to Pythagoras, he almost said. Because of you. What he said instead was, "Most of the book is worthless. Maybe you can help me save the rest?"

She looked at him for a long moment, considering more than this offer, more than the work of helping with the book. Considering why she had interrupted him on the green, why they kept meeting. Why they kept walking away somehow more alive but less satisfied. "Let me read it," she said. "Then we'll see."

On the plane, everybody treated Duane differently than he was used to. They avoided him, but they weren't giving him any of the rookie treatment, either. There was a respect. They weren't afraid of him, exactly, but – he could feel things had changed. At least until they were waiting to take off. Then Coach stood up at the front and did his thing.

"We did what we needed to do," he said. "We stole one on their floor. Now we defend our home court with everything in balance." Coach acknowledged Duane first: "Duane, you were phenomenal." Duane shifted in his seat, uncomfortable, but then Coach said what everybody knew – "That kind of performance is a gift. It's not going to come every night." Duane imagined they were all thinking about game one, how bad he had looked.

Then Coach said what he always said: "This is a team. We're in this together. We work together, we dream together, this is *our* moment." Coach never wavered, he always sounded like this was the first time he was saying it. He meant every word, every time. Duane saw Chris across the aisle, nodding his head, his eyes closed, like he was praying. The Believer, he thought. Basketball was religion to that man. Coach said: "We came into this season, nobody even had us in the playoffs. We're in *Vegas*, still you couldn't find a bet in our favor." Leroy, sitting next to Duane, chuckled. He was nodding too, like Chris, but his eyes were wide open, looking around. Shoulders high, chest out... Looking proud to be one of them. It hadn't been like that much of the season.

Coach said: "It's the peak of opportunity, gentlemen. The precipice, right before you fly or fall." Coach was poetic, thought Duane. He could be over the top. But he was what they needed... They all needed inspiration. Coach couldn't be out there with them on the floor, but he could give them hope, guidance, strategy, inner strength. Maturity, too... They were kids, most of them, just kids.

"We are men," said Coach, defiantly, like he had read his thoughts, like he was arguing with him, and Duane smiled. Coach was good. Coach said: "You are men of character and fortitude. You showed that in Houston. Let's show that at home. We'll hit the details in practice, but... Good job, guys. But be ready for more. Be ready, Highrollers. Be committed, be smart, be courageous. One game at a time."

And when he sat back down things were back the way they had been. Leroy took his pillow, didn't even acknowledge him when he did it. Duane was a rook; he didn't say anything. It was the natural order. He figured next year he'd be treating rooks pretty much the same.

Game three, Houston at Las Vegas. Most of the pre-game show was spent on rising star Duane Dimes, popularly known as D-Squared, and featured in-depth analysis of his incredible performance to close the previous win. They cut between replays of his top season highlights and close-ups of him warming up on the floor. Gary thought Dimes looked nervous. Ben was hoping for a repeat performance, but from Dimes' expression, Gary didn't think it was likely. It looked to him like the pressure was getting to him already, like it was going to prove too much.

"I can't believe you got rid of that tape," Ben said. "A title this season would have been really something. Legendary."

"It can still happen," said Gary, but Ben shook his head.

"It would be a miracle." The TV displayed a close-up of Dimes warming up with mid-range jumpers. Making most of them, but still, he looked distracted. Body language wasn't good. Shaking his head, stretching his hands, looking at them like he doubted their ability to work. Ben said, "It's better, though, without the tape. I really want to be a Dimes fan, you know? So if he's going to do it he's got to do it on his own. I can't be helping him with a time-traveling tape every game."

"I wish you wouldn't talk about the tape," said Gary.

"Please," said Ben. "We'll be talking about that tape forever. I won't tell anyone else, you have my word on that. But to not talk about the craziest, weirdest, not to mention coolest experience in our lives?" He sighed. "It's just too bad we won't get to tell our future wives. Not that I'll ever have one. I don't know if I could marry some girl honestly, you know, carrying a secret like that." The TV image changed to slow motion highlights of Dimes in the previous game. Gary's favorite was one where Dimes grabbed the rebound and led the fast break, then finished on a put-back slam when McDaniels missed the layup. With a tone of reverence, Ben said, "We changed history. I can't believe it. I don't know why you didn't give it to your professor."

"I explained my reasoning," said Gary.

"He seems like a stand-up guy, though," said Ben.

"He is," said Gary. "I haven't told him anything about it, yet. Maybe I will at some point, I don't know. We just started working on the paper today. We're still going to replicate the experiments, just the way we planned. That's enough for now, that's all. One thing at a time."

"Right," said Ben.

Gary sighed, wishing Ben would let it go, wishing Ben would understand – Gary didn't know if he had done the right thing. "I don't understand it," he said, "and that's the real problem. We did something... I mean, I know what we did, step by step, but I don't know how it caused the tape. It's an item of mystery, and I doubt it would be unraveled before it would be used for all the wrong purposes." Ben's expression – half-grin, half-shameful hanging of the head – said he agreed. "You asked if I could make another one. I can't.

I don't really know I made it. Maybe once I understand that, how it was actually accomplished... When I can make it again, not by luck or accident but by *design*, then that will be how I know it's safe to use it."

"You'll make another," said Ben, confidently.

Gary shrugged. He didn't know. He couldn't see the future.

For days, Will struggled to distract himself, unable to get his mind off the memory of the Artifact. He was at a loss to explain what had happened, what he had experienced. For a thousand years he had been trapped in the Garden of Eden. He had given Rick the impression that he had spent those years alone, after the man and the woman – Adam and Eve – had left; and in a way that was so. But he had many companions. It had been a Garden empty of people but full of wildlife, strange and inexplicable. Things he recognized but did not understand.

He remembered a fox with red fur that had stopped and peered into his face, screaming long howling barks, insistent about something he could not decipher. The fox had been a regular visitor for far longer than any fox could have lived. There had been a monkey that had first run up behind him and swung from above, as though holding onto the Artifact, clawing at his eyes, as though he could scratch through the helmet and damage the skin beneath. He too hollered and danced as though frustrated that Will could make no sense of his message. He too returned again and again, immortal and unchanging through all that time. Strangest of all had been a hummingbird that a thousand times flew around him again and again, singing merrily, but only once had stopped, directly in front of him. It hovered in front of his eyes, close enough to fill his vision, and he saw that on its back rode a tiny butterfly. The two were like one, the still wings of the butterfly rustling ever so slightly from the fluttering breeze of the hummingbird's wings, beating endlessly, effortlessly, too fast to see. The butterfly was marked with strange eyes upon its wings, a rainbow iris around violet pupils, like it too wore a mask, one that seemed to be looking at Will, measuring him, small movements of the wings making the pupils expand and contract.

He had tried to speak to all these creatures. He had begged for help. In his loneliness he had told stories of his life, shared all his hidden thoughts. If they heard them they did not know how to reply.

They were trying to tell him something, he knew, that he could not understand, not for a thousand years, and now, he didn't want to understand. He wanted to go back to his humdrum life and forget these dreams of the mysterious and impossible.

He tried to lose himself in work. He called choir members, asked about their lives. He made his way to Pastor Drew's office for philosophical conversation. He went through binders of hymns and praise music, planning Sundays months ahead.

He tried to lose himself in music, in Rabalyov, whose complex, tragic puzzles surely would insulate him from his own. But it was no use. Rabalyov today seemed old and tired, a voice of another world, whose vital spirit had long since fled, or been crushed by the weight of its own ponderings. He tried Chopin, Debussy, Bach.

He called his family. But he couldn't speak of what he had experienced. He had never told them of Rick's secret Artifact – and how could he ever now? Instead he worried them by calling with nothing to say. He listened to his sister's music cues – she had broken through her resistance and had no time to talk, but she had sent each in an e-mail as soon as she had finished. They were excellent, full of life and vigor, and he was happy for her success, but he himself remained uninspired.

He was angry at Rick for deleting the video file. He couldn't blame him, and he knew his reaction was silly; anyway, what could the video reveal? A few hours of footage at most, if it had captured anything at all.

But Rick, in typical fashion, hadn't asked for his opinion. And Will wanted to see it. Wanted to see that it was real. It was impossible, the unimaginable time that had passed. He had started to think Rick was right – it was a thing of imagination, a thing of mirages and false visions. Why had he ever thought the Artifact revealed truth?

It didn't matter now. The Artifact was gone, and he had already returned the recording device to Dave. "How did it work out?" Dave had asked, and he had brushed it aside.

"No time to use it," he said. "Didn't want to keep it from you if I wasn't going get a chance to try it out." The way Dave looked at him, the little frown, the dipped brow, he must have known he was keeping something from him, but Dave was not the prying type. He had taken it back without comment.

When Dave called him three days later, Will was restless, depressed, frustrated, with no conceivable outlet. He felt traumatized, with a secret no one could understand or comprehend. Dave said on the phone, "How you doing, Will?" and Will couldn't respond. All he could get out was a word, "Yes," not an agreement, just a sound to confirm he had heard.

"It's about this camera," said Dave, then, quickly, "don't say anything yet. When you first got it back it was acting a little funny. Normally I would ask, I guess, did you experience any... problems? You know, with its use, but..."

"I'm sorry," said Will, desperately, "if I broke it."

And Dave, on the other end of the phone, chuckled, a soft sound, but a sound somehow full of depth and kindness. "Oh it's not broken," said Dave. "Broke is *not* the word. But just listen–" so Will didn't say anything "–one of the things I did was, I went in to the file system and restored a deleted video. *I'm* sorry about that, Will. I mean, that I did that, invaded your privacy like that."

"What do you mean restored?" asked Will.

"Well, I undeleted it," Dave said. "Easy to do, since no one had recorded anything over it. Resurrected it from the lost clusters."

"You watched it?" said Will.

There was a short silence, then that soft chuckle again. "Still watching it, more like," said Dave. "It's been going since yesterday." He waited a second, but Will didn't say anything. Dave said, "Will, the file size keeps changing. I've never seen anything like this before. I wouldn't have thought this was possible, Will. It's like it's streaming... like it's streaming straight from the device. The device can only hold *two hours*, Will." Then, "I even fast-forwarded for... I don't know how long. It seemed like an eternity." In his voice was a hushed awe, a sense of mystery that said he, like Will, had been unable to sleep, unable to stop thinking about it. "It's you wearing it, right?" Dave said. "I heard your voice."

"Yes," said Will, his voice tight. "Yes, it's me."

"I can't stop watching it," Dave said, like it was a confession. "I know I should, but I'm afraid… I'm afraid to mess it up." He paused. "I thought you might know," he said. "How long does it go?"

And now Will was the one to chuckle, a nervous sound, like it shivered out of his chest in fear. "So long," he said. "You could never watch it all." There was a silence on the other end. In the background, Will could vaguely hear the sound of a voice. He recognized it as his own, calling to someone. "Please, help me," he heard himself calling, and he was ashamed, ashamed for Dave – or for anyone – to hear the lost, abject loneliness in that sound.

He didn't know what to think. He didn't know what Dave wanted. He didn't know what *Will* wanted. "Stop it," he said. "Can you delete it again?"

Dave heard the pain in his voice, but still hesitated a moment. "Are you sure?"

And in that moment… "No," said Will. "No, don't. I'm coming over."

"Good," said Dave, relief in his voice. "I was hoping you would say that."

When the keeper of the Garden of Bliss discovered what Adam and Eve had done, that they had tasted of the tree of the knowledge of creation, he sent the two of them away.

"Because you have listened to the voice of your wife," he said, *"and have eaten of the tree about which I commanded you, 'You shall not eat of it,' cursed is the ground because of you. In toil you shall eat of it all the days of your life."*

It was the first they had ever known of hardship and sadness. They hungered, they thirsted, they experienced illnesses of the body and mind. It became nearly unbearable for Eve, with changes and sickness that seemed not meant for her small frame.

But later, after she had given painful birth to a son, there was nothing but pride and joy in her eyes. Adam, during the struggle, worried for Eve as he never had before. But when the baby's tiny hand wrapped tightly around his finger he too was overcome with joy more refined, more potent, than the bliss of the Garden he had lost. He named him Cain, for the gift they had acquired through pain.

"Look what we have done," Eve said to him, in wonder, her face transformed. "We have made a man."